446, 961 star
iball

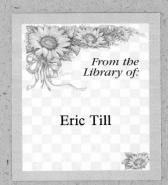

GOD BLESS US
EVERY ONE!

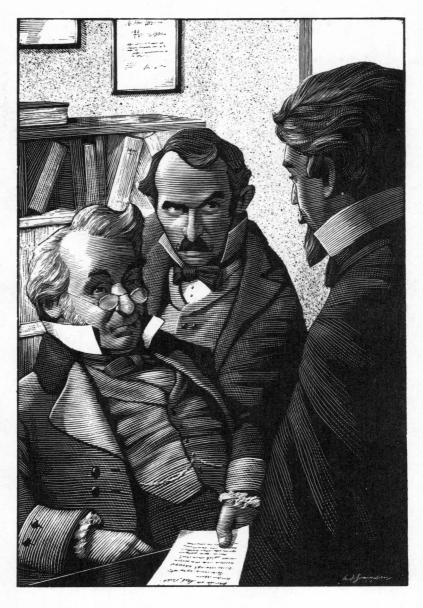

"And we happen to believe," said Hall, "that this story of 'A Christmas Carol' is the most beautiful that we have ever heard."

GOD BLESS US EVERY ONE!

Being an Imagined Sequel to
"A Christmas Carol"

ANDREW ANGUS DALRYMPLE

⋂ METHUEN
Toronto New York London Sydney Auckland

CANADIAN CATALOGUING IN PUBLICATION DATA

Dalrymple, Andrew Angus, date
  God bless us every one! : being an imagined
sequel to A Christmas carol

ISBN 0-458-99430-8

I. Title.

PS8557.A47G62 1985   C813'.54   C85-098818-7
PR9199.3.D248G62 1985

DESIGN: Pronk & Associates
ILLUSTRATIONS: Mark Summers
COMPOSITION: CompuScreen Typesetting Ltd.

Printed and bound in Canada
by John Deyell Company

1 2 3 4   85   89 88 87 86

for ELFIE
my wife
— with love

CONTENTS

PREFACE

I have endeavoured in this Sequel to the greatest of all
Christmas stories to place myself and my readers in early
Victorian London on Christmas Eve, 1843, at the very
time when young Charles Dickens and his band of
"Christmas Carol" companions were just starting off on
their march down the ages.

In making this attempt, I trust that I shall not put
Dickens's legion of admirers out of humour with themselves, with each other, with the season, or with me.

And may they—and Dickens!—forgive me.

A. A. D.

CHARACTERS

EDWARD CHAPMAN, a noted publisher.
JOHN VINE HALL, Mr. Chapman's partner.
GEORGE GAMESTER BLOGGS, Chapman and Hall's clerk.
DUDLEY DUGDALE, Chapman and Hall's printer.
CHARLES DICKENS, a rising young author.
CREEP, butler to Mr. Robert Cratchit.
DAISY WELLBELOVED, Mr. Cratchit's maid.
MRS. SUMMERHAYES, Mr. Cratchit's cook.
EUSTACE FONSDALE, Mr. Cratchit's driver.
LORD POUNCEY, chairman of the Yorkshire Penny Bank.
HORACE HUDDLESTON, an official of the Home Office.
ROBERT CRATCHIT, a prosperous businessman.
MRS. CRATCHIT, the worthy partner of the above.
BELINDA, the Cratchits' youngest daughter.
TIMOTHY("Tiny Tim"), the Cratchits' youngest son.
EBENEZER SCROOGE, a kind-hearted, jovial old
    gentleman.
DR. ERASMUS YOUNGBLOOD, physician to Mr. Scrooge.

MRS. GUBBINS, a former housekeeper to Mr. Scrooge.

YOUNG MAN IN STREET, known to Mr. Scrooge seven years previously.

NOEL AXWORTHY, Master of Paradise Hall.

GLORIA AXWORTHY, wife of the above and receptionist at Paradise Hall.

ZACHARY MAKEPEACE, a turnkey at Paradise Hall.

TESSIE WITHERSPOON, an inmate of Paradise Hall.

HAMISH WROTTENBURY, a newspaper reporter from Glasgow, Scotland.

BARTHOLOMEW HOSKINS, Mr. Dickens's driver.

SIR ROBERT PEEL, Prime Minister of Great Britain.

CAPTAIN LOCKHART, an officer of the 2nd Mayfair Dragoons.

HERCULES, Mr. Cratchit's trusty horse.

1

A Calamity Indeed

George Gamester Bloggs was puzzled, to begin with. Nothing quite like it had ever happened before. He sat at his desk in the front office of Messrs. Chapman and Hall, publishers (where he had worked happily for seventeen years, though he had nothing at all to do at that moment), and his puzzlement was quickly replaced by a feeling of apprehension—in less than a minute he would be positively alarmed.

Christmas Eve in London in the year 1843 began as a mild and sunny morning with just a trace of snow on the rooftops and lingering ice on the window-ledges. Indeed, had Bloggs been forewarned that the day would be so unusually balmy, he would have left his heavy topcoat and his muffler, to say nothing of his gloves and winter boots, at home.

But I'm afraid it wasn't the weather that was exercising Bloggs's mind as he sat at his desk and worried. He was listening to the mournful voice of Mr. Chapman, who was reading from a sheaf of papers—actually, a manuscript—and who was addressing his partner, Mr. Hall, on the far side of a nearby frosted-glass partition. As he listened, Bloggs nervously watched their silhouettes on the glass and unmistakably saw Mr. Hall raise his handkerchief and dab at his eyes as the moving peroration continued.

"Algernon trembled," Bloggs heard Mr. Chapman read, "and got a little nearer to the ruler. He had a momentary idea of knocking Flintlock down with it, holding him, and calling to the people in the court for help and a strait-waistcoat.

" 'A merry Christmas, Algernon!' said Flintlock, with an earnestness that could not be mistaken, as he clapped him on the back. 'A merrier Christmas, Algernon, my good fellow, than I have given you for many a year! I'll raise your salary, and endeavour to assist your struggling family, and we will discuss your affairs this very afternoon, over a Christmas bowl of smoking bishop, Algernon! Make up the fires, and buy another coal-scuttle before you dot another i, Algernon Muddlecombe!'

"Flintlock was better than his word," Mr. Chapman went on. "He did it all, and infinitely more; and to little Lame Joe, who did NOT die—"

It was here that an alarmed Bloggs heard Mr. Hall give a distinct half-sob, not at all the sort of sound the clerk was accustomed to hearing in a business-house such as this.

"—he was a second father. He became as good a friend, as good a master, and as good a man, as the good old city knew—"

Bloggs stopped listening and jumped to his feet. A confident and buoyant gentleman sporting a door-knocker beard and a swirling cape had entered from the street; he was in his early thirties—to be precise, he was thirty-one—and he carried a metal despatch-case. His eyes fairly gleamed with anticipation, and his lips bore what may well be described as an excited smile.

"Good morning, Gee-Gee!" the newcomer exclaimed, for this was how George Gamester Bloggs was popularly known. "Are the presses rolling yet?"

The clerk bit his lip and glanced at the partition. The visitor followed his gaze, frowned, and strode to the office door, but Bloggs beat him to it, opening the door just in time.

"Mr. Dickens!" he called out, announcing the young author, and withdrew.

"Well, gentlemen?" Charles Dickens demanded even before the door had been closed behind him. "I honestly thought I'd hear your presses rolling by now!"

Chapman and Hall rose and gravely shook their heads. Chapman, the portly one, lowered the manuscript he had been reading and placed it on the desk. The lips of Hall, the morose and thin one, still quivered tremulously.

" 'Twon't do, Mr. Dickens," Chapman began. "Will it, Mr. Hall?"

" 'Twon't do," agreed his partner sadly. "It needs work, Mr. Dickens."

"Needs *work*? That's the most wonderful story I've ever written! And every word of it is true! Do you mean to tell me you reject it?"

"Only as it stands," said Chapman.

"We'd like some changes made," added Hall.

"I refuse to change a word!"

Chapman opened a drawer and pulled out a second manuscript. "No, just the names. Now in this first draft of yours, the one you let us have when the old man first told you his story, Mr. . . . er, Mr. . . . er—"

"Scroggins, wasn't it?" suggested Hall.

"It was Scrooge!" retorted Dickens.

"Scrooge, yes," said Chapman, glancing at the pages. "Now I put it to you, Mr. Dickens, and my partner heartily agrees with me"—for Mr. Hall always did—"that the names of Scrooge and Cratchit are infinitely more effective than those of Flintlock and Muddlecombe."

"And we hate," cut in Mr. Hall, "the new name you've given to Tiny Tim—Lame Joe!" He pursed his lips in disgust.

"But," protested Dickens, "I can't use the actual names of these people! I mean, it simply wouldn't be fiction!"

"But it *isn't* fiction, is it?" countered Chapman. "Tell me, where does Mr. Scrooge live, Mr. Dickens?"

"I don't know, I didn't ask him. But Bob Cratchit has an office, Mr. Scrooge told me that, somewhere in Threadneedle Street." The young author lifted his door-knocker beard thoughtfully; instead of gleaming, his eyes began dreaming. "The real names, eh?"

"And we happen to believe," said Hall, now unashamedly wiping his eyes, "that this story of 'A Christmas Carol' is the most beautiful that we have ever heard."

"It will be a privilege to publish it." Chapman, for once, was agreeing with his partner. "I predict a fortune, a fortune for us all."

"When do I get my money?" Dickens was eager again: ever since his days as a boy in the blacking factory, and later, as a newspaper reporter, he had always been a true professional.

Chapman and Hall smiled. Chapman then handed Dickens the original manuscript he had taken from the drawer and patted the author's arm encouragingly.

"Get us those *real names*, Mr. Dickens—permission to use them! They're better than anything you've yet invented!"

"Quite so," agreed Mr. Hall.

Bob Cratchit's house in London's Mountjoy Square bespoke the fact that he had come high in the world, for his stately residence on the corner was a mansion, with its own little mews adjoining. Passers-by hurried; most carried Christmas packages. Wheels clattered over the cobblestones as a street-vendor, pushing a handcart bearing the sign "Digweed's Fruits," called, "Christmas oranges, penny a dozen! Mixed nuts, best nuts for Christmas!" Two boys, their mufflers flying, jostled a gentleman as they raced by him, but if you believe for one moment that the gentleman was Charles Dickens making for Bob Cratchit's house, you would be mistaken. It would take the young author, unfortunately for him, at least an hour and a half to discover where Cratchit lived and get there. Perhaps it was just as well; otherwise, we would have a much slimmer story, probably no story at all, as the momentous events I am about to relate would simply not have occurred had Dickens known where Cratchit lived and gone there immediately. Of this I am certain.

No, the man who was jostled by the scampering lads was a pompous fellow indeed, Lord Pouncey, and he was accompanied by a circumspect official named Horace Huddleston. The pair glowered after the boys, then marched up the steps leading to the Cratchits' front door. His lordship banged on the door with his silver-topped stick, scraped his boots on the rail, and waited. And banged. And waited.

Inside the house, which was dressed for Christmas, the front hall and living-room were deserted. Over the fireplace there hung a portrait of Scrooge, and beneath it, displayed like a sporting-gun, a crutch. As Lord Pouncey renewed his assault on the door, Creep, Bob Cratchit's butler, came in slowly from the corridor—the poor old chap was about sixty-five and wore a butler's uniform complete with faded white gloves.

During his plodding progress to the front door, and as the pounding continued, Creep paused when he reached the sideboard and poured himself a quick glass of sherry. He was about to drain the glass when Daisy Wellbeloved, a cheerful young parlour-maid of about twenty or so, appeared at the top of the stairs leading up from the servants' area in the basement.

"Will I answer it for ya, Mr. Creep?"

"No, thank you, Daisy, I can manage."

Unlike Daisy, who had a strong Cockney accent, Creep was blessed with a West of England twang, as used by the early Americans. Those from England, that is.

"Oh, lor'," exclaimed Daisy, on seeing Creep gulp his sherry, "Christmas izzen 'ere yet, y'know."

"Back downstairs, Daisy, where *your* business is," Creep remarked, not unpleasantly, as he proceeded at some speed to the door. "Mine's upstairs."

Daisy grinned and went down as Creep opened up.

"Good morning, gentlemen."

"We wish to see Mr. Cratchit. At once." Lord Pouncey peremptorily dumped his things on Creep's chest, as did Horace Huddleston.

"I'm afraid the master hasn't returned yet, gentlemen."

"We'll wait." Lord Pouncey thrust one of his large, gold-edged calling-cards between the butler's teeth.

"Oh, yes, my lord," gritted Creep, glancing down. "Thank you, my lord."

But the visitors had already gone to the fireplace, where, despite the mild day, they showed their behinds to the fire and rubbed.

"Would you care, gentlemen," enquired Creep, having

also peremptorily dumped their things on the hat-stand, "for me to announce you to my mistress?"

"Mrs. Cratchit? May as well." Lord Pouncey looked approvingly around the room as Creep, now with the calling-card on a small silver tray, made off down the corridor. "Well, this Cratchit has certainly done as well as they say, Huddleston."

"Better, my lord, perhaps better. One of the richest men in the city, by most accounts."

"And in spite of his past associations. Well, all credit to him."

"Indeed, my lord, though Cratchit's the one who doles out credit these days." Huddleston turned from the fire and glanced up at Scrooge's portrait. "Excuse me, but isn't this old Scrooge himself?"

"That's him, the bounder. Oh, the honest men he put out of business in his time, including my own father! The men Scrooge ruined in his infamous career! 'Twould be better now for Cratchit if old Scrooge were dead."

"Perhaps he is, my lord, with any luck."

"I'm afraid not; we should have heard. The passing of even a reprobate like Scrooge would not have gone unnoticed in the city."

"Fancy hanging Scrooge!" said Huddleston, referring to the portrait.

"There are many, Huddleston, who'd fancy it very much."

Creep doddered in from the corridor. "I'm afraid I can't find Mrs. Cratchit, gentlemen, she isn't in the sewing-room or the conservatory."

At this moment a shrill voice was heard from upstairs: it was Mrs. Cratchit, and she was coming down.

"Creep! Creep! Have you seen my chocolates?" Mrs. Cratchit came into view, revealing herself to be rather plump, somewhat over-dressed, and wearing too many trinkets; but jolly, withal. "Ah, there you are, Creep," she said as Creep approached her, proffering the card on its tray. "I can't find my chocolates, the hard-centred ones."

"They're in the living-room, madam, together with two visitors."

Mrs. Cratchit gushed at the card and hurried over. "Oh, Lord Pouncey! Oh, my lord!"

"At your service, madam," said Lord Pouncey, bowing slightly. "May I present Mr. Horace Huddleston of the Home Office?"

"Charmed, madam." Huddleston oozed insincerity. "Charmed and delighted."

"Creep! Serve the sherry." Mrs. Cratchit motioned the visitors to sit as Creep returned willingly to the sideboard.

"We went first to your husband's place of business, ma'am," explained his lordship, "but were informed he was not there."

"Oh, no, he wouldn't be, my lord. Not on Christmas Eve."

"Ah, no doubt, ma'am," interposed Huddleston, and his next remark caused Mrs. Cratchit to become doubtful indeed, "this being the eve of Christmas, your husband is out visiting the poor and deserving."

"That may well be. But I expect him quite soon now."

Lord Pouncey gave a sidelong look at Creep as the butler clinked the sherry-glasses. "We have news to impart, madam, that is highly confidential."

"Serve the sherry, Creep, and then leave."

"If I may say so, madam, that's an odd decoration." Lord Pouncey was clearly making small talk until the butler had disappeared, but he hastily clarified his remark on seeing that Mrs. Cratchit had glanced down at one of her trinkets. "Over the mantel, I mean."

"The portrait of Mr. Scrooge?" Mrs. Cratchit accepted a glass of sherry, as did the visitors. "Oh, no, we like it."

"No, I mean what's immediately beneath it. It seems to be a crutch of some sort."

"Crackers, madam?" enquired Creep solicitously.

"What did you say?"

"With the sherry."

"We require no crackers, Creep, that is, unless . . ." Her visitors shook their heads. "That will be all."

Creep made his way to the servants' stairs, where he stood in his butler's place and listened, unobserved by the others.

"As a matter of fact, Lord Pouncey, that *is* a crutch," remarked Mrs. Cratchit when the three had sipped. "I know it's rather odd to hang such a thing over the fire, but that crutch serves as a memento to all of us of much harder times. That crutch, I'm afraid, belonged to one of my sons."

Lord Pouncey tried to look concerned. "Dear me, that's too bad. And the poor boy died, did he, madam?"

"Oh, no, Timothy was saved, and by a wonderful, wonderful man!"

"We are most pleased to hear it. Who saved him, madam?"

"Timothy now walks as straight as the proverbial arrow. He was saved seven years ago—it was about this time of year, I think—by a kind old gentleman who took Tiny Tim, as we called him then, under his wing."

"Such enterprise should be rewarded!" exclaimed Pouncey.

"I believe I can say he has already had his reward, sir."

"Who, ma'am?" asked Horace Huddleston.

"Doctor Wunderkind of Geneva." Mrs. Cratchit sipped a little more sherry.

"Geneva, Switzerland? The famous Doctor Wunderkind?"

"Oh, yes, and he was most expensive, I can tell you. Took Tiny Tim into his hospital, kept him in the Alpine air, soaked his leg for months in the invigorating salts and waters of the area, and Timothy came home to us after a year completely cured. It was awfully costly, but most worthwhile." Mrs. Cratchit put down her sherry-glass, the better to clasp her hands. "And Timothy will be home from boarding-school at any moment. My daughter, Belinda, has gone to meet him at the station. Think of it, gentlemen! He'll be home for Christmas!"

Even as his mother exclaimed these words, Tiny Tim, who was now fourteen years old and who had become, therefore, a somewhat troublesome teenager, was being greeted by his sister at a busy ticket-barrier on Paddington Station, which was bedecked with streamers and wreaths of holly. A crush of arriving passengers, all eager to be home for Christmas, pressed round. A military band on the station's concourse blared "Joy to the World," a rendition marred only by the hiss and chuff of departing steam-trains and the piercing whistles being blown by the guards. Tiny Tim embraced Belinda, now a pretty eighteen-year-old, with affection, and the two, followed by a porter bearing a school-trunk with the initials "T.C." on his shoulder, pushed smilingly through the crowd in search of a hansom-cab—but not too smilingly, for Tiny Tim was worried.

And before their mother had picked up her sherry-glass, a carriage was arriving in Mountjoy Square. Inside sat its owner, Bob Cratchit, looking prosperous and somewhat self-satisfied. When the carriage arrived at his front door, Cratchit climbed out, smiling and holding a box wrapped in Christmas paper. His driver, Fonsdale, handed down his master another package from the driver's seat, this time a large, mis-shapen one. Cratchit beamed, hurried down the outside basement steps, and entered the kitchen, where he presented the larger package to Mrs. Summerhayes, the cook, and at the same time patted it knowingly. He then went up the servants' stairway and discovered Creep at his post, eavesdropping. Although he admonished Creep as he went up, Cratchit was quite good-natured.

"Out of the way, Creep. Go up and take my things."

"Oh, certainly, sir. Beg pardon, sir."

Mrs. Cratchit rose upon hearing their voices, as did her visitors. "Ah, here's my husband now. Not like him to use the tradesmen's entrance, I can tell you."

She greeted her husband at the top of the stairs, where Cratchit cheerfully kissed her. "There you are, my love. I gave Cook the grandest piece of pork, a gift from Twilly. And these are for you, handmade bon-bons from Mrs. Twillingpost. Gin and rum in 'em, gin and rum!"

"Oh, thank you, Mr. Cratchit, and we have visitors!"

"Pouncey! My dear Lord Pouncey!" Cratchit strode over and jovially shook his lordship's hand. "And a merry Christmas to you, my lord!"

"The same to you, sir. This gentleman is Mr. Horace Huddleston, of the Home Office."

"The Home Office!" Cratchit took the Home Office's hand. "Well, welcome to my home! I trust my wife has kept you entertained."

"Most adequately, sir," lied Huddleston. "We called at

first at your office in Threadneedle Street, but your chief accountant informed us you were out. Probably, as I just suggested, you were visiting the—"

"I've been visiting my racehorses down in Epsom to see how they've been wintering. They're doing remarkably well!"

"But I had no idea," observed Lord Pouncey as everyone sat down and Mrs Cratchit busied herself opening her new box of chocolates, "I'd no idea that you own a string of racehorses!"

"Hardly a string, my lord," Cratchit replied amiably, "only seven. And I hazard a guess, which comes straight from the mouth of my trainer, Twillingpost, that my filly, Pandora, will win the Littlewick Stakes at Epsom next year."

"Pandora, eh?" Lord Pouncey thoughtfully tapped his brow. "One worth noting, eh, Huddleston?" Lord Pouncey put aside thoughts of future riches and pulled himself together. "And now, Mr. Cratchit, now for our news. We have come directly—well, almost directly—from the residence of the Prime Minister himself." Lord Pouncey frowned as Mrs. Cratchit dug his ribs with her chocolate-box, then smiled, took one, and put it in his mouth. "Ah, thank you, madam. Perfectly wonderful news."

Huddleston, similarly tempted, yielded at once. "Delightful news; delicious."

"Affecting me?" queried Cratchit as his wife happily nibbled. "What does Sir Robert Peel want this time?"

"It isn't . . . what the Prime Minister . . . wants, my dear Cratchit," Pouncey chewed, "it's what he is prepared . . . to give. Tell him, Huddleston."

Huddleston pulled an official-looking scroll of paper from his inside pocket. "It's all here. For your services to business and more especially to the Tory party, your name is to be put forward for inclusion in Her Majesty's New Year's Honours List, one week hence."

Cratchit was suitably stunned. "You don't mean a knighthood?"

Pouncey and Huddleston nodded and smiled as sagely as they could.

"I shall be Sir Robert Cratchit! And you, my dear, will be a lady!"

"Oh, at last! Those donations of yours have truly been rewarded!"

"I must caution you," said Lord Pouncey, who by now had swallowed what was left of his rum-soaked date, "to treat the news as strictly confidential." (Creep, of course, was listening more intently than ever from his place on the stairs.) "Any indiscretion," Lord Pouncey went on, "any leakage, could lead to a withdrawal of the bestowal. Queen Victoria always likes to be first with the news."

"Lady Cratchit!" exclaimed the future Lady Cratchit.

"Sh!" shushed the others, except Creep.

"Lady Cratchit." The worthy partner of the future Sir Robert whispered the words with relish.

"No indiscretion of any sort," counselled Lord Pouncey, as Creep, who had evidently heard enough, sneaked down to the kitchen on tiptoe to tell Daisy, the maid, and Mrs. Summerhayes, the cook, all about it, also that they might all be able to look forward to a small increase in salary. "Thank heaven," Lord Pouncey continued, "that your old partner, Ebenezer Scrooge, no longer dares to show his face in the city."

"Who?" Cratchit's response was so utterly vague and his face so decidedly blank that it was almost as if he'd never heard of his great benefactor.

"I said Ebenezer Scrooge."

"Oh, him. Yes, well, the old fellow is pretty much over

the hill nowadays, he's content to see me as the senior partner in the firm of Cratchit and Scrooge. He's no longer active, I'm afraid."

"D'you mean," Lord Pouncey asked eagerly, "that the old skinflint is as good as dead?"

"Mr. Scrooge dead?" echoed Cratchit, his lips at the same time trying to form themselves into the semblance of a smile.

Mrs. Cratchit laughed loudly at the mere notion of such an idea. "Mr. Scrooge? Oh, no, not Mr. Scrooge! Not Mr. Scrooge, my lord!"

It is fortunate for us that Mrs. Cratchit was so outspoken, for her words carried into the adjoining cloakroom behind the front door, where, next to a rack on which hung the family's hats and coats, there was an old bed with bed-curtains. One of these bed-curtains was now grasped and swished aside, and Ebenezer Scrooge, now seventy years old, came into view upon hearing his name. He wore a dressing-gown, a long night-shirt, a night-hat, slippers, and spectacles perched way down his nose; he carried a copy of the morning newspaper, which he had been reading while resting on the bed, but had subsequently dozed off. He now limped, for he was in considerable pain, to the cloakroom-door, where he listened, cupping one hand around his ear, his expression changing from approval to disgust as he heard what was being said in the living-room.

"I would strongly recommend, if he is still alive," Scrooge heard Lord Pouncey say, "that you get him off the company's business title as soon as possible. After all, it used to be Scrooge and Marley, then it became Scrooge and Cratchit, and now it's Cratchit and Scrooge. In view of his unsavoury past"—Scrooge now looked slightly resentful—"it may be a good idea to get rid of his name altogether. Call it Cratchit and Company." Scrooge scowled.

"Oh, I don't know if I could quite do that, my lord," Cratchit said. "And he changed his ways, you know, seven years ago. Had a dream of some sort."

"Yes," said Mrs. Cratchit, "when he woke up, his mind had gone funny. He sent us round a duck, if I remember rightly."

"No, it was a turkey, my love ... I think. And the following day, Boxing Day it was, he gave me an increase in pay, and later on he made me his manager. Since then I've never looked back. Oh, I could never delete him from the firm's business title, my lord." Scrooge smiled on hearing these words and began to nod in appreciation, but before his first little nod had been completed, his old face fell as Cratchit continued, "Not while he's alive. When he's dead, of course, I might well consider changing it."

"But if you're to be Sir Robert Cratchit," said Pouncey, "with a knighthood"—Scrooge clutched his face and shook with laughter—"the old man's past may soon catch up with you. There are many, still, who hate and detest him. Everyone who ever knew him, for example." Scrooge was crestfallen.

"Where does he live, Mr. Cratchit?" Huddleston enquired.

"Far away from here, I'll be bound," his lordship ruminated before Cratchit had a chance to reply. "Probably in hiding somewhere. It's a wonder to me that he's not in jail."

Cratchit ventured, somewhat awkwardly, "Well, as a matter of fact, he has a little room overlooking the mews around the corner. He's crippled with gout—"

"How dare he have the royal disease?" Lord Pouncey was most indignant.

"Well, he has it," Cratchit admitted, "that's why he can't get upstairs. That's why, I'm afraid, we moved him in here."

Lord Pouncey was astounded; he gaped, then jumped to his feet. "In here?" he bristled. "Do you mean Scrooge lives here, sir, with you?"

Cratchit became timid. "He's in the little cloakroom adjoining."

It was Huddleston's turn to rise. "Scrooge lives in a cloakroom?"

Bob Cratchit and his wife thought they, too, had better stand. "Yes, we thought it best," said Mrs. Cratchit, wondering why her visitors now resembled goldfish. "I do believe he's quite happy there."

"Thank goodness," Pouncey exclaimed, "*my* coat isn't hanging in there! Tell me, can he hear us?"

"Oh, no, my lord." Mrs. Cratchit was quite mistaken. "He's a bit hard of hearing occasionally."

"And I know he's happy," remarked Cratchit, trying to make light of the whole thing. "He lives rent-free. He has no interest whatever in making money these days."

"But my dear sir," said Pouncey, "as soon as you are knighted, shoals of important people will be coming to see you! Influential new friends, lords and ladies—like me! The presence of Scrooge will be a constant embarrassment! What will people think," his lordship demanded to know, "when they see his dreadful face over the mantelshelf, then find him in with their hats and coats? Some of his old enemies will very likely murder him in there! And you, sir, will be shunned forever. At this stage of your career, the slightest whiff of scandal . . ."

Pouncey's voice trailed off despairingly as Huddleston

took his cue. "I fear this may well affect the Prime Minister's decision."

"To say nothing of the Queen's!" The ball had bounced back into Pouncey's court. "They do say that in his day Scrooge even swindled Prince Albert!" Scrooge's face twitched behind the cloakroom door, and on hearing Pouncey's next remark, he became horrified. "You should move Scrooge out of the house, Mr. Cratchit, send him to a home for the elderly!"

"But we can't do that," Mrs. Cratchit protested. "The poor old man is nearly dead now."

"May we see him?" Lord Pouncey was eager again. "And satisfy ourselves?"

On hearing that those in the living-room were about to come into his quarters, Scrooge quickly sat down in his little armchair, threw a travelling-rug over his knees, placed his newspaper on his lap, closed his eyes, and pretended to sleep.

"We *had* called, you see, Mr. Cratchit," said Huddleston evasively as the four approached Scrooge's door, "merely to acquaint you with the Prime Minister's *proposal* to put your name before Her Majesty, to ascertain if you would accept the honour that may or may not be accorded to you. It's quite unofficial."

"Oh, but I do accept! I do!"

"Yes, well, when we inform Sir Robert Peel of the presence in your home of a man who was once an unmitigated monster—and we shall be obliged to tell him—I'm very much afraid he may well withdraw your name, and you may remain a Mister."

"Unless something is done, and quickly!" Pouncey reminded Cratchit.

"Do let me show him to you, my lord." Cratchit opened the cloakroom door, and the quartet trooped in. Scrooge

"What a cunning old devil," exclaimed Lord Pouncey. "He's nowhere near being senile."

closed his eyes more tightly and gave out with a little snore. "You will observe that he's quite harmless these days."

"There, you see?" Mrs. Cratchit smiled again as she gazed at the slumbering figure. "The poor old gentleman is like a little baby."

"He's very weak," Cratchit ventured. "He reminds me of a Covent Garden vegetable."

"Yes," said Lord Pouncey, for once agreeing with his host, "like one you might see in the gutter. Rotten to the core."

"Should I wake him up, I wonder?" Cratchit asked naïvely.

"But of course! I want to see if he's well enough to be moved!"

Mrs. Cratchit responded earnestly and quietly to Pouncey's outburst. "My lord, I should never want to see Mr. Scrooge leave this establishment. We owe the old gentleman so *much*."

"Mr. Scrooge ... Mr. Scrooge..." Cratchit touched Scrooge's shoulder to no avail, then shook him vigorously. "Wake up! You have visitors!"

Scrooge opened his eyes and asked, very faintly, "Who is it? Who, sir? Who? Is it time for my beef-tea?" Scrooge looked up at Cratchit, appearing not to notice the others. "Bob Cratchit, my dear and faithful old friend. I haven't seen you for months. Is Christmas over yet?"

Lord Pouncey jabbed his finger at the newspaper on Scrooge's lap. "He knows it isn't! Look, he's reading today's newspaper. What a cunning old devil. He's nowhere near being senile."

"Who's there?" Scrooge peered into the middle distance. "I hear someone else."

"It's Lord Pouncey," Cratchit explained, "chairman of

the Yorkshire Penny Bank. Distinguished member of the Worshipful Company of Silversmiths."

"But I don't understand, Bob." Scrooge was making a valiant attempt to appear dense. "Why would anybody want to worship a silversmith?"

"See, his mind is going," Mrs. Cratchit volunteered, "if it's not completely gone."

"It's all an act, ma'am," Lord Pouncey averred spitefully, "I know this villain of old." His lordship then shouted directly into Scrooge's startled face, and with quite surprising vehemence: "Now you listen here, Scrooge! You need something this house can't give you! A complete rest, elsewhere!"

"A complete rest?" Scrooge responded nervously. "Oh, I shall be getting that soon enough, sir."

Pouncey, not without a note of triumph, turned to Cratchit. "See, he's as sane as you are. I suggest you get rid of him immediately, and for a week at least until the list comes out. If society discovers you are harbouring this outcast, you can bid any award—shall we say?—farewell. You can always bring him back in the new year; January or, better still, February. But if you will take my advice, if you let him return, you will board him up in the attic. If he's crippled with gout, as you say, he won't be able to get *downstairs*, either."

"We have no desire to seem harsh," Horace Huddleston confirmed, and if his listeners inclined to the opinion that he was speaking officially on behalf of the mighty Home Office, if not Her Majesty's entire government, their assumption would have been a correct one. "A week or two away from here should be sufficient, until the award is a *fait accompli*. Then, perhaps, the attic."

Creep, the butler, had taken advantage of the fact that the

sherry-drinkers had gone into Scrooge's room: what more opportune moment, he had concluded, having heard the sound of their footsteps overhead, to go up to the living-room with his little silver tray, clear away the glasses, and refresh himself at the sideboard? Creep had barely re-charged Lord Pouncey's glass and drained it when the front door opened and Belinda Cratchit came in.

"Hello, Creep, my brother's just paying off the cab. Would you please help Timmy with his things?"

Creep hurriedly lowered his lordship's glass, swished and swirled the sherry around in his mouth, then gulped, "With pleasure, Miss Belinda." He tottered into the street to help carry in Tiny Tim's school-trunk.

Bob Cratchit, on hearing his daughter's voice, came out of Scrooge's room with the others, leaving Scrooge disconsolate and alone. Scrooge's door was closed.

"Lord Pouncey, may I present my daughter, Belinda? Belinda, this is Lord Pouncey and Mr. Huddleston."

Both Pouncey and Huddleston were charmed and impressed, for as well as being pretty, Belinda was vivacious, and the two men murmured that this was indeed the case.

"I was thinking of having a small supper-party this evening to celebrate your, uh, news, my lord," said Cratchit as his wife went into the living-room to fetch her chocolate-box, "and was hoping that you and Mr. Huddleston might care to attend."

Pouncey glanced at Scrooge's door. "Will he still be—?"

"Leave that to me."

"Then I shall be delighted. It will be such a pleasure to see Miss Cratchit again." Mrs. Cratchit waddled toward them, carrying her box. "And of course you, too, my dear Mrs. Cratchit."

Huddleston agreed, "And so shall I be happy, Miss Cratchit!" He added, with much less enthusiasm, "And Mrs. Cratchit."

Cratchit beamed as he looked towards the open front door. "And here's my son, Timothy! Home for the holidays!"

Tiny Tim and Creep came in, struggling with the trunk. The boy immediately put down his end, removed his cap, and rushed over to his mother. "Mother! Father! Oh, Mother, it's so good to see you again!" He kissed her. "How's Uncle Scrooge?"

"Uncle Scrooge?" Pouncey echoed incredulously.

"It's just a term of endearment," Cratchit explained, "you have my word he's no relation. Lord Pouncey, Mr. Huddleston: this is my son, Timothy."

"Ah, the one who didn't use to walk straight," Lord Pouncey remembered, taking the boy's hand. "And where are you being educated, my little man?"

Tiny Tim's reply was decidedly awkward. "Well, I've been at Cavendish College, my lord. Before that I was at Blakewell, and at Cottlestone Manor."

"Three of the finest preparatory schools in England!" Lord Pouncey gushed. "Your son must have a great brain!"

Cratchit replied witheringly and with great doubt, "Yes."

Tiny Tim suddenly remembered an urgent engagement elsewhere and backed away. "Excuse me, sir, I'll just help Mr. Creep, if I may."

Before he could do so, Mrs. Cratchit popped a chocolate into her son's mouth. Tiny Tim grinned, picked up his end of the trunk, and started up the stairs with Creep. Belinda also made for the stairs. "And if you'll excuse me, too, gentlemen," she said.

"Charmed and delighted," said Huddleston.

"We were just leaving," said Pouncey.

As the visitors took their things from the hat-stand and small table, assisted by Cratchit, Tiny Tim turned on the stairs, beckoned with his free hand to Mrs. Cratchit to come up, and hissed conspiratorially: "Mother! Mother!"

Mrs. Cratchit nodded and smiled at her visitors, then went upstairs behind Belinda.

"And if you can tell me tonight that the deed has been done," said Lord Pouncey, with a nod at Scrooge's door, "I shall be obliged to you, Cratchit."

"The Prime Minister will be so relieved," said Huddleston, putting on his muffler.

Lord Pouncey tapped the top of his top-hat into place and pointed to the fireplace. "And I should get rid of that portrait, if I were you," he advised Cratchit. "Seeing that face over the fire is most embarrassing."

"Embarrassing indeed," confirmed Huddleston, as Cratchit opened the front door. "Good day, sir. Until tonight!"

Cratchit smiled, closed the door behind them, and turned; deep in thought, the future knight rubbed his hands contentedly.

Scrooge, in his room, was worried indeed. He rose and clasped his hands, then called out quietly to various parts of the ceiling. "Jacob! Jacob Marley! I need you, Marley! It's me, Ebenezer!" Scrooge looked around expectantly, then shrugged sadly when the ghost of his old partner did not appear.

After a brief tap on his door, Daisy, the maid, came in with a tray. " 'Ello, Mr. Scrooge. 'Ere's ya lunch. Nice mug o' beef-tea an' a biscuit." She placed the tray on Scrooge's small table.

"Daisy!" exclaimed Scrooge, brightening—though not

from the sight of his lunch. "Just the girl I need! Could you go to my old house in Mincing Lane and ask Mrs. Gubbins to come here? Tell her it's most urgent!"

"Won't 'ave time before lunch, guv."

Scrooge pulled a coin from his dressing-gown pocket. "Go by hansom, there and back. Here's a shilling. Please, Daisy."

Daisy softened, gave him an understanding smile, and accepted the coin. "All right. If it's urgent."

"Thank you, Daisy. Bless you."

Daisy hurried out. Scrooge sat at his table, sipped his steaming beef-tea, picked up the large biscuit that was his main course, and inspected it ruefully.

"Creep! Come down here." Bob Cratchit had come to a decision. He stood at the foot of the stairs, gave a little glance of appreciation at Daisy as she went down to the servants' area, and waited impatiently for Creep to descend. "Coming, sir," Creep called, and came down.

"I want you to go to Paradise Hall in Little King William's Alley."

Creep cringed, wringing his hands. "But isn't that the workhouse, sir? Oh, please don't send me there, I beg of you, Mr. Cratchit! Not yet."

"I'm not sending *you* there, you idiot. In any case, it's only partly a workhouse, it's mainly a rest-home. I want you to tell Mr. Axworthy, the Master, to come here. Tell him there's a delicate matter I wish to discuss."

"Yes, but what about luncheon, sir?"

"Will you stop asking me questions, Creep?" Cratchit fished a coin from a crack in his well-stuffed waistcoat. "Here's a shilling. Go by cab."

"Very good, sir." Creep's eyes glinted and registered fourpence, an amount he knew he would save if he made the downhill part of the journey on foot, an amount sufficient to buy half a tumbler of gin in the Mucky Duck Inn on the way back. "At once," Creep dutifully told his master as he went eagerly downstairs for his coat. But Cratchit had already gone to Scrooge's room and opened the door.

"Mr. Scrooge! I wonder if you'd mind coming in here for a moment."

Scrooge came out, limping painfully. "Into the *living*-room?" He followed Cratchit, touching for support the tops of chairs as he plodded. "Well, this must be an occasion, Bob."

"It will be. Come over here to me, by the fire."

"Ah, Bob," said Scrooge, gazing down into the flames, "do you remember that Christmas Eve seven years ago when I was too mean to give you a little lump of coal? Now look at your fireplace, Bob, it makes me so very proud of you."

"Do you wish to sit?"

"No, thank you, I think I'll stand."

There was an awkward pause as Scrooge raised his eyes from the fire and looked up at his portrait. He gripped the back of Cratchit's armchair. "And do you remember, Bob, on that Christmas Day, referring to me as you toasted me in your little home as being the Founder of the Feast? And such a little feast!"

Cratchit winced. "I'm afraid I can't quite recall—"

"Oh, I was with you, Bob. In spirit."

"Do you mind if we get back to reality for a moment?" Cratchit, although mildly testy, was not too unpleasant. "And will you kindly stop vexing me by harping on things I don't wish to remember? Now look here, old chap. I have an extremely delicate business matter coming up in the next few days, and it would benefit me very much if you were out of the house. You will be well taken care of, I promise."

"May I thank you for all you've done for me, Bob?" Scrooge couldn't help but sound fairly pathetic, but he added bravely, considering his age, "Where do I go?"

Cratchit's reply brought a wistful, far-off look to Scrooge's eyes; it was almost as if he recalled using similar words in the past. "Have you no relations? Have you no friends?" Scrooge shook his head. "It's just for a few days."

"And days grow into weeks and months," Scrooge reflected. "There's my nephew, Fred, but he entered Parliament—I always said he would—and naturally he doesn't want to acknowledge *me* any more. No, I have no home, except here, but I do want to see you happy, Bob, you and your family. I'll go, I'll be glad to."

Cratchit softened and reached out to touch Scrooge's arm. "No, damn it, I don't believe I can go through with it. I'll not see you go. Please forget the entire matter."

Scrooge moved slightly away so that Cratchit's hand did not reach him; he wanted to save his old clerk from any feeling of embarrassment.

"Is it a matter of great importance to your career?" Scrooge asked, knowing that it was. "Is it? You must tell me."

Cratchit said nothing, but hung his head and nodded.

"Then I'll not prevent it," said Scrooge, drawing himself up and taking his hand from Cratchit's chair. "But one favour, Bob," Scrooge said earnestly as he started for his room. "Please don't send me away . . . before Christmas."

Bent and hobbling, Scrooge approached his cloakroom door, followed by a rather concerned Bob Cratchit. "May I offer you some money, to tide you over?"

Scrooge smiled as he grasped the door-handle. "No,

thank you, I gave most of mine away. It's odd how giving people money makes them happy, and me, I'm happier without it. But I still have a few sovereigns left." He opened his door and went in, repeating as he did, "A few sovereigns."

But on the other side of the door, once he had closed it, there was a different Scrooge. He leaned back against the door, took a handkerchief from his dressing-gown pocket, removed his spectacles, wiped his eyes, and blew his nose. He then sadly lifted down from a peg on the wall an old black suit of clothes on a hanger and slowly began to get dressed.

Mrs. Cratchit and Tiny Tim came bustling downstairs. Both looked worried. In her hand Mrs. Cratchit held a letter. "What your father will say I do not know! It's the third time, Timothy!"

"What's the third time?" Bob Cratchit glowered, coming over. "Don't tell me he's been—"

Tiny Tim interrupted his father, a shade defiantly. "Yes, I've been expelled again, Father."

Mrs. Cratchit handed her husband the letter. "Don't be too hard on him, dear."

"Hard on him?" Cratchit scowled as he read from the letter aloud. " 'Refuse to tolerate your son any further'? . . . 'Indolent and insolent'? . . . 'A bad influence on other boys'?" Cratchit lowered the letter and clenched it, his face reddening. "This is the third time in eighteen months! Is no school in England good enough for Master Timothy Cratchit? At your age I was working, earning half-a-crown a week! Oh, the disgrace! If this gets about . . . My knighthood!"

"What knighthood?" asked Tiny Tim innocently.

Cratchit, furious, grabbed Tiny Tim's ear and pulled

him across the room. "Don't be impertinent, sir! You and I shall have a talk! In the library!"

He dragged a cowering Tiny Tim into the library and slammed the door. Mrs. Cratchit sighed and, to console herself, sat by the fire and nervously nibbled on a bon-bon.

The hansom Creep had hired for part of his journey turned into Little King William's Alley, a mean street not far from the Tower, narrow and drab. Few people were about. The cab stopped outside a gloomy, gaunt building with great iron gates topped with spikes. The old servant was most apprehensive about visiting such an establishment, and he licked his lips as he glanced up and took in a soot-covered sign nailed high on the wall:

PARADISE HALL
Loving Care for the Elderly
—and All Other Unfortunates

But when Creep entered the building, using a side-door a few yards from the main gates, he was relieved. He found himself in an office, a reception area, that was sumptuous and palatial. The appearance was deceptive, but Creep could have no understanding that this was perfectly normal in such places as this, so that prospective inmates could more easily be enticed in. Nor could Creep know that once past the reception area an awful Victorian slum, with all its attendant horrors, lay beyond. Bob Cratchit also had no idea.

Creep went over to a high reception-desk fitted with a grille, behind which an ugly and avaricious woman, who later in this narrative will prove to be Mrs. Axworthy, was scratching a quill pen dipped in thin ink across a thick registration book. She looked up on hearing Creep give a little professional cough; then she squinted and half-smiled, revealing a Queen's highway paved with potholes and generally ill-fitting teeth.

" 'Ell ... lo," she said speculatively, and from her manner it wasn't clear whether she regarded the butler as yet another prospective inmate or a likely corpse, for she continued, " 'Oo are you? Funeral parlour's round the back, dear."

Creep swayed, and for once it wasn't the result of anything he'd been drinking.

Belinda Cratchit, having removed her bonnet and tidied her hair, came listlessly downstairs and approached her mother in the living-room.

"Oh, Mother, will I be compelled to attend Father's supper-party this evening? Must I be present?"

"Of course you must! Don't *you* start, young lady!"

"But I never meet anyone young! Father wants me introduced only to men of position. Power, Mother, and rank. Middle-aged gentlemen of influence and wealth."

Mrs. Cratchit rose, the better to rebuke her daughter. "And look how well it helped your sister, Martha, and your brother, Peter! They both married well, thanks to your father."

"But they both married *old* people," Belinda pouted. "Oh, Mother, I don't want to share the same fate! Why, you yourself were married at my age, and Father was but two-and-twenty! But now see him! He insists on guarding me as though I were a crown jewel of some sort."

Mrs. Cratchit smiled and took her daughter's arm. "You are, my dear, you are, and very soon *this* crown jewel may well be presented at Court. Come into the sewing-room, Belinda, I have a very confidential matter to impart."

The two went down the corridor to the sewing-room, and, as they did, two other women came upstairs from the servants' area: one was Daisy, who had a finger to her lips, admonishing her companion to remain quiet; and the other was a dowdily but respectably dressed woman in her fifties, Mrs. Henrietta Gubbins, a ripe, engaging Cockney. Daisy tapped on Scrooge's door, and the two entered.

"I got Mrs. Gubbins for ya, Mr. Scrooge." Daisy then withdrew, closing the door.

"Mr. Scrooge!" Mrs. Gubbins greeted him boisterously and with great affection. "Oh, it's so good to see you again, fair warms me cockles!" She kissed him on the cheek. " 'Ow are you, then?"

Scrooge, having dressed, buttoned up his jacket and smiled. "Thank you so much for coming. I still have the gout rather badly, Mrs. Gubbins, but more important than that, how are you?"

Mrs. Gubbins spread out her hands delightedly. "Riddled through an' crippled with everything, my dear! My oldest friends are lumbago, sciatica, and rheumatiz, they've settled in an' are doin' nicely, thank you, an' I 'ad a stabbin' new pain this mornin', just arrived, Arthur Itis, I think 'is name is, 'e gave me such a wallop, right up my back."

"You must tell me all about it some time," said Scrooge, sitting down with her at the table.

"Now wot's this urgent thing you wants me for? Anythin' wrong?"

"You remember, Mrs. Gubbins, how clever you were at reading the tea-leaves?"

"Oh, is that all you want? Want me to read a cup now an' tell about yer future prospects?"

"No. I also remember, when you looked after me in

Mincing Lane, your remarkable skill in dealing out the playing-cards and gazing at the ball."

"But wot's so urgent about wantin' yer fortune told?"

"That still isn't it," Scrooge replied. "What I should like you to perform is another one of your tricks. I need to contact someone in the spirit-world. Kindly conduct one of your justly famous seances. Only this time bring me Jacob Marley."

Mrs. Gubbins was most surprised. "Your ol' partner? The one 'oose ugly mug you thought you saw on my door-knocker?"

"Yes," Scrooge admitted, "I need his advice most desperately. He came to see me seven years ago this very day, and I've been trying to bring him back without success. I don't need him so much myself," Scrooge went on, "but I'm terribly worried about Bob Cratchit, and I've an idea that Jacob will know what to do. You see, Cratchit intends to turn me out of his house."

Mrs. Gubbins, in her indignation, thumped on the table with both her fists. "Your ol' clerk! Wot a rotter! Tell you wot, why don't you come back to yer old 'ouse in Mincin' Lane! It'll be you an' me together, just like the old days. Oh, I'll look after you, all right! An' you can rub my back for me!"

But Scrooge failed to react favourably to this proposal. Instead he pursed his lips and remarked, "Er, no, much as I appreciate your gracious offer, I think I prefer to see what Cratchit has in store for me. Meantime, kindly invite Mr. Marley to join us."

Mrs. Gubbins spread out her hands in consternation. "At this time o' the day? Wot the spirit world wants is darkness, darlin'."

"I'll close the curtains, then." Scrooge rose and pulled

the curtains across a small window in the cloakroom's alcove overlooking the mews. His room now went so dark that Scrooge and Mrs. Gubbins could not see each other at all.

"If Marley and his friends can change me," Scrooge said, stumbling back to his chair, "they can transform Bob Cratchit, too. Now let me see."

"Where are you, love?"

"Ah, here it is." Scrooge sat down. "What happens next?"

"Give me your 'ands. Both of 'em."

"Right. There you are."

"Oo, Mr. Scrooge!" Mrs. Gubbins was elated. "We're 'oldin' 'ands! In the darkness!"

"So I perceive. That is, so I am aware."

"Now wot we want to do now is wait for the rap," Mrs. Gubbins explained, trying to sound mysterious. "I want to 'ear somethin' knockin' under the table."

"This should be most interesting."

"It should start bangin' away in a minute or two, with any luck. Now let's you an' me concentrate for a bit. Wot a seance needs is dead silence."

This would have been all right had Mrs. Gubbins observed her own regulations governing the conduct of successful seances, but she didn't. Instead she suddenly shouted at the top of her voice, causing Scrooge to wince and Creep, who had come up from the servants' area and entered the living-room, to perform the quickest change in facial reaction he could muster as he gaped twice at Scrooge's door.

"Don't move, Mr. Scrooge!" cried Mrs. Gubbins. "Shut yer eyes, keep 'oldin' my 'and, an' we'll 'ope for the best!"

Creep gulped, walked away, and opened the library

door, from behind which he had already heard Cratchit's angry voice. Cratchit was shaking Tiny Tim vigorously by the shoulders, at the same time shouting, "And I shall tolerate no more of this conduct of yours at *any* school!" On seeing Creep, Cratchit came storming up to the door. All he said to the butler was an irritable "What?"

"Oh, sir," Creep began diffidently, "I went to Paradise Hall, but I'm afraid I was unable to give your message to Mr. Axworthy. You see, sir, he had to go to a hanging."

"A hanging?" Cratchit was incredulous. "On Christmas Eve?"

"Well, they didn't want to have it on Christmas Day, sir."

"Did you leave my message?"

"Indeed, sir. Mr. Axworthy will attend on you directly."

Creep's reward for imparting this information was to have the library door slammed in his face. He turned, rubbed his rubicund nostrils, went over to Scrooge's door, and tapped three times.

"That's it!" Mrs. Gubbins called out triumphantly. "There's the rap we've bin waitin' for!"

"Good old Jacob," Scrooge exclaimed approvingly, "I knew he wouldn't let us down." It was Scrooge's turn to call out loudly. "Is that you, Jacob Marley?"

"It's me, sir. Creep," said the old retainer, entering, the light from the living-room revealing that Scrooge and his lady-friend were indeed holding hands. "Is everything all right?"

"No, you've ruined everythin'!" protested Mrs. Gubbins, and referring to the marked reluctance of Jacob Marley to materialize, she added, with some disgust, "I'll never get 'im to come now!"

"I'm terribly sorry, madam," apologized Creep.

"Wait!" Mrs. Gubbins wasn't done yet. "Sit down with us an' 'old 'ands! Another man in the room should improve things."

Scrooge noticed Creep's hesitation and encouraged, "It's perfectly all right. This woman is my former house-keeper."

Creep cringed again. "But I don't think I feel quite up to it, sir!"

To Mrs. Gubbins's delight a loud knock was heard.

"There it is! A spirit is approaching!"

"Sounds to me," said Creep, turning, "more like the front door, madam." He went to answer it.

Mrs. Gubbins rose, holding her head in frustration. Scrooge also rose and opened the curtains in his little alcove.

"Oh, it's no use," said Mrs. Gubbins, acknowledging defeat. "I can't go on. Y'see, the best seances only 'appen at night when the spirit-world is roamin'. I'll come back this evenin', late, an' I'll entice ol' Marley 'ere even if I 'ave to drag 'im by 'is chains."

"May I count on that, my dear Mrs. Gubbins?" Scrooge blinked his old eyes as the winter sun streamed in again.

"Yes, 'cos if I can't do it, I'll get one o' my late 'usbands to fetch 'im. We often 'as a chat."

Creep had opened the front door and admitted a stranger, a fine young fellow indeed—he was tall, well dressed, handsome, and had an exceedingly engaging smile, but if you believe that here, at last, was the long-awaited arrival of that famous young author, Charles Dickens, then I am afraid I must disappoint you, for at this particular moment Dickens had just left Bob Cratchit's office in Threadneedle Street, having ascertained the address in Mountjoy Square where Cratchit had his residence, and was striding impatiently this way and that, looking in vain outside "The Old Lady of Threadneedle Street" (as Londoners affectionately refer to that august institution, the Bank of England) for a hansom-cab to convey him to Mountjoy Square. Luckily for us, on that busy Christmas Eve Dickens would have a long wait. And when he did get a vehicle, to his increasing anger it would be pulled by the slowest horse in London, for Fate had stepped in and decreed that Dickens would arrive at Bob Cratchit's mansion at precisely the wrong moment.

No, the dashing fellow whom Creep had allowed to step smartly across his master's threshold was about twenty-eight and carried a shiny new doctor's bag. After taking his hat and gloves, Creep took the stranger to Scrooge's room, where Mrs. Gubbins was making ready to leave.

"Mr. Scrooge, is it?" enquired the young man, in whose open features were generously combined the qualities of humour, tolerance, sympathy, and understanding. "I am Doctor Youngblood."

"Oo!" cried Mrs. Gubbins with a good deal of pleasure, for she, quite naturally, much liked the look of this young fellow. "That's a good name for a doctor!"

"Yes." With a shy and charming smile, Dr. Youngblood placed his bag on Scrooge's little table and addressed the old gentleman. "I'm the locum for Doctor Lovejoy. He's away for Christmas, but before he left, he asked me to be sure to come to see you."

"Extremely good of you, Doctor," said Scrooge gratefully and politely. (And say what they might about Scrooge, he was always very polite, even when he was addressing Creep, which he was now about to do.) "Creep, would you be kind enough to take Mrs. Gubbins downstairs to the kitchen and offer her a nice cup of gin before she goes?"

Creep proved to be willing. "It will give me much pleasure, sir."

Mrs. Gubbins began to follow Creep from Scrooge's doorway. "Thank you. See you tonight, Mr. Scrooge! Look after 'im, Doctor!" And when Creep had closed Scrooge's door, she asked him, "Wot sort o' gin 'ave you got?"

"Cream of the Valley, madam," advised Creep, indicating the lower stairs. "It's a beautiful gin."

"It killed my third 'usband, it did," said Mrs. Gubbins, delightedly rubbing her hands in anticipation. "Revenge!"

The two went eagerly down to the kitchen.

"Yes, Doctor Lovejoy told me about your gout," said the young Doctor Youngblood, proudly opening his new doctor's bag, "and I've brought along for you a totally new remedy. It's a potion of my own invention." He produced two small jars, each containing a thick, white liquid, to which were affixed two neat little labels bearing, after the usual medical gibberish, the immortal name "Erasmus Youngblood, M.D."

"Now these two jars," Dr. Youngblood went on, "should tide you over the holidays. Take one full spoonful whenever you can't move. I'll be eager to know if it works."

"Well, I can barely move now," said Scrooge, reaching for the spoon that reposed in his empty beef-tea mug. "What *is* this stuff, Doctor?"

"It's difficult to say, exactly—that is, in lay terms. I've been spending a few weeks with a veterinary-surgeon friend down in Sussex, and we've been doing some experimenting."

"A vet, you say?" Scrooge unscrewed the top from one of the jars and sniffed eagerly. "Well, if the *animals* like it, it may work on a man who was once considered a beast of the city." He dipped in the spoon and tasted, then observed, smacking his lips, "H'm, it does have what you might call a bucolic quality."

"That's because it was used during the recent outbreak of foot-and-mouth disease."

Scrooge hastily swallowed the remainder of the generous dose he had poured himself.

"I've seen it work wonders," Dr. Youngblood went on confidently, "on a herd of cows and an elderly stallion; the pain in their legs was relieved considerably. Do you know something, Mr. Scrooge?" The young doctor smiled what was probably his most disarming smile as he snapped his new bag shut and prepared to leave. "You're the first human being on earth to try this new potion of mine. I'm so hoping it will help *homo sapiens*."

"Me, too, Doctor." Scrooge opened his door, looked down, and couldn't help but notice that he was still hobbling. "Well, thank you for coming, I hope I see you again." He ushered Youngblood into the living-room. "There's a lot of gout about, you know. I was reading in the paper only this morning that some of the highest people in the land suffer from it. I shall be glad to be your, guinea-pig."

A near-collision was only narrowly averted, for just as Scrooge and Youngblood came through the cloakroom's doorway, they almost walked into Mrs. Cratchit and Belinda as they hurried past Scrooge's door to the stairs. Not even the sagest of sages knows for sure when love will strike, and if Belinda and the good doctor had been advised in advance that this would occur, they would undoubtedly have discounted such a notion. But they believed it now, in the moment that their eyes met, becoming, as they did, instantly infatuated and falling deeply in love on sight; they did not know it, but they had been waiting all their lives for each other. I should add, merely for clarification, that Mrs. Cratchit, being a woman, also heartily liked the look of this handsome fellow.

"Oh, forgive me, ladies," said Youngblood, gazing down in his manly fashion into Belinda's burning eyes, and wishing that the narrowly missed collision had taken place. "I beg your pardon."

"Ah," Scrooge smiled, astutely observing the young people's infatuation, "may I present Mrs. Cratchit and her dear daughter, Belinda? This is Doctor Youngblood."

"Erasmus," the young man stressed. "Erasmus Youngblood."

As he said these wonderful words, the doctor couldn't help but marvel as he examined Belinda's breathless smile and perfectly formed lips. And he noted, not without satisfaction, that while she made no reply, those same beautiful lips now seemed to mouth the simple word "Erasmus," though, as I have already mentioned, what she actually said was nothing.

"He's helping Doctor Lovejoy," said Scrooge encouragingly.

Youngblood leaned forward and stooped, or, to put the gesture in another way, he gave an elegant little bow.

"Mrs. Cratchit . . . Miss Cratchit . . . I understand that as well as Mr. Scrooge, the Cratchit family are also Doctor Lovejoy's patients."

"And I've been so poorly lately, Doctor!" Mrs. Cratchit gurgled. "Proper poorly!"

"Tell me," Erasmus Youngblood, M.D., asked silkily, plunging into his role as family-physician and friend, "do you ever eat chocolates, Mrs. Cratchit?"

"Occasionally." Mrs. Cratchit may have become all girlish and coy, but she had no idea that Youngblood was about to give her the best medical advice she'd had in years.

"Well, it's my prognosis that you should eat more of them. They'll buck you up, good for energy. You should stuff yourself."

"Oh, but I do!" She hastily corrected herself. "I mean, I shall!"

"And if you, ma'am, or your daughter, ma'am," Youngblood went on, filing away in his mental reference-file the fact that Miss Cratchit had the most exquisite teeth, a fact he intended to ponder a little later, "if either of you should ever desire a personal consultation, I shall be glad to be of service. I sincerely hope that Doctor Lovejoy will take me on as his permanent assistant."

"And so do I!" Mrs. Cratchit almost shouted the words. "What say you, Belinda?"

"Oh, yes!"

Scrooge decided he would do his utmost to assist the young lovers. "Doctor Youngblood has just given me a new cure for my gout. Tell me, are you all alone in London this Christmas, Doctor?"

"Yes," said Youngblood, noting that Miss Belinda was lovingly hanging on his every word. "Alone and unattached, I'm afraid."

"All alone, and single, too!" Scrooge said, for emphasis. "We can't have that on Christmas Eve! Would you care to join me tonight for a little late supper?"

"Why, yes, I'll be glad to. Thank you, sir."

Creep crept from nowhere to the hat-stand and picked up Youngblood's hat and gloves. Youngblood took both the hint and his things with quite good grace, in the circumstances, and as Creep opened the front door, to show he was definite about returning Youngblood remarked fervently, "Until later, ladies." Then he went out.

"Oh, Mother," said Belinda as the two watched Youngblood raise his hat to them in the street, "could we not ask Father to let him join the party tonight?"

"I'll do more than ask him, my dear!" said Mrs. Cratchit, sincerely regretting that Creep had now closed the front door. "I'll *tell* him." She turned to Scrooge. "Tiny Tim is here, you know."

"Tiny Tim?" Scrooge was hurt. "But he hasn't been to see me!"

Mrs. Cratchit touched Scrooge's arm, for she knew her words would genuinely affect the old man. "He's been expelled again."

"Oh, the poor boy. I must speak to him."

Mrs. Cratchit nodded and went over to the library with Belinda. "Let's see if your father has finished with him. And we'll tell him about that young doctor. He'll be as thrilled as we are!"

The two went into the library, where Cratchit was still shaking Tiny Tim and shouting, "And if this happens again, I'll flay you, understand?" The library door then closed behind them, so what happened in there next it is impossible to know.

That most expert hoverer, Creep, now decided to get something off his grease-stained chest: he would tell Mr. Scrooge of his mission to Paradise Hall, and in the most dramatic of terms, thus compelling the kind old gentleman's rapt attention. "Oh, sir, I have some urgent news to relate, if I may. If you only knew the name of the individual I was ordered to send for this morning. If you only knew!"

To Creep's amazement Scrooge permitted his usual politeness (which we have already noted) to desert him. "I neither know nor wish to know!" Scrooge lifted his left foot. "My gout is going!" He lowered his left leg, then raised the right. "I believe I can walk!" He ventured a step or two. "I can! The pain's been entirely relieved! Look at me, Creep! Observe!" Scrooge was so elated he gave a hop and a running jump, then performed a brisk little dance all around Creep while the astonished retainer looked on.

"I can hop, I can dance!" Scrooge sang. "I'm as merry as a schoolboy! Merrier! I thought to jump and run were distant memories! The potion! It works, Creep!"

"You're a treat to see, if I may say so, sir."

"You may! You must! My gout has got up and finally gone! That young and handsome doctor did it! Bless him! And you, Creep! You admitted him!"

Scrooge held both hands aloft and glided swiftly through the doorway of his room while Creep shook his head in wonder.

"I must share my good fortune," Scrooge called as he disappeared into the room reserved for hats and coats and which, as you are aware, also served as his humble quarters. "I must share my good fortune with a dear lady who suffers greatly from similar aches and pains. She must have it within the hour!" Scrooge fairly hurled himself into the chair at his little table, snatched pen and paper, and began to write. "Wait while I write this note! You can take her the other jar!"

"But I can't, sir," said Creep, peering through the doorway. "Luncheon will soon be served. I'm sorry, sir."

Right on cue Daisy, that most efficient and pert little maid, came scurrying up the servants' stairs with a tray piled with several covered and steaming dishes.

"Well, Daisy must take it," said Scrooge as he scribbled. "That good little girl will do anything I ask of her."

"Don't look at me!" ejaculated Daisy, sailing past his door. "Come on, Mr. Creep! It's feedin'-time."

Creep darted to the dining-room door so that Daisy could continue sailing, held it open, and followed her inside.

"Ah, well," said Scrooge, deftly applying blotting-paper and rising, "I suppose I shall have to see to it myself." He picked up the second jar of potion and came out of his room babbling happily to himself. "But I must relieve that dear lady's suffering. Good for horses? Good for me!" He broke into a half-gallop as he approached the front door. "I can do more than just walk! I can run! I'm as frisky as a colt! Why, I do believe I could even—" Scrooge did not explain further whatever it was he believed he could do, for he had reached the front door and opened it; he now peered eagerly out, his eyes swivelling up and down the street. "Hey, boy! Come here, boy!"

Scrooge called to a dejected young man of about eighteen who was walking slowly and aimlessly by with one foot in the gutter and both hands in his pockets. He wore an old cap at a rakish angle and was, generally speaking, quite sloppily dressed. He looked over at Scrooge, who was urgently beckoning to him to approach, entirely without interest and with a slight feeling of irritation that his brooding reverie had been interrupted.

"Yes, you, boy! Come here! Most kind of you!"

The young man shambled over and looked at Scrooge with dark suspicion. "Wotcha want?"

Scrooge took a coin from his jacket and handed it, the envelope, and the potion to the moody young man. "Would you be kind enough to take this jar of medication to the lady whose address appears upon the envelope?"

The young man glanced reluctantly at the envelope, then at the coin. "Think I'm goin' all that way for 'alf-a-crown? There?"

This remark caused Scrooge to glance at the young

man keenly. "Wait a moment," he said as awful recognition began to flicker in his old eyes. "Wouldn't you be the same young fellow I asked to run and buy a turkey some seven-odd years ago?"

The same awful recognition welled up in the young man's eyes, causing his frown to deepen into a scowl. "Wouldn't you be the same ol' geezer 'oo doesn't know wot day it is? You *are*, ain'tcha?"

"What an intelligent boy, a remarkable boy! And to think of it, now you're a young man, a delightful young man, it's a pleasure to talk to you. Now I'd like you to run as fast as you can, and—" Scrooge extracted a second half-crown from his jacket pocket and pressed it into the young man's hand "—here's an additional half-crown for you to spend on the way back. But don't," Scrooge counselled the remarkably intelligent young fellow, "don't go stopping in any gin-shops or ale-houses on the way there! That lady is desperately waiting!"

"All right, guv," said the young man, clinking the coins, "for five bob I'll do it for ya." Scrooge nodded and smiled and began to close the door, but the young man prevented this by placing his hand against it. "An' by the way," he reminded Scrooge, "if you're not quite sure abaht it, today is Christmas Eve."

"Brilliant, brilliant, I'd almost quite forgotten," said Scrooge, closing the door when the young man had removed his hand from it. "Grateful, most grateful."

The young man trudged away as slowly as before, then turned and ambled off in another direction. It was as if he did not intend to deliver the envelope, or the medication, at all.

Scrooge had just closed the front door and was about to return to his room when the library-door was thrown open and a fuming Bob Cratchit thrust Tiny Tim, now thoroughly shaken up and sobbing quietly, into the living-room. "Up to your room and stay there until sent for! Move, sir!"

Cratchit gave his son the sort of shove only a father can give, sending the lad scurrying across the living-room in the direction of the stairs. Cratchit then went back into the library, where Mrs. Cratchit and Belinda were waiting to tell him all about the lovely young doctor the family had just acquired.

And at the foot of the stairs was Scrooge. He had watched what had happened with concern, and he now crouched, throwing out his arms. Tiny Tim, tears streaming down his face, came running straight into Scrooge's embrace. "Oh, Uncle Scrooge! Sometimes I wish I was a cripple again! I do!"

Scrooge, too, appeared on the verge of tears, but made a determined bid to answer the boy brightly. "There, there, Tiny Tim, I know what it is. Your Uncle Scrooge knows what's troubling you. But you must respect your father's wishes and go upstairs, now mustn't you?"

He stood up straight and took the boy's hand. "Did your father say you had to be alone in your room?"

Tiny Tim shook his head.

"Well," said Scrooge, "let's go up together and talk it all over, shall we?"

The two began to go up. Tiny Tim brushed his eyes with his other hand and was quite incredulous. "But Uncle Scrooge! You're walking upstairs! Walking *upstairs*!"

"I know, Tiny Tim," Scrooge smiled, "isn't it wonderful? I've a new medication, brought to me by a young doctor, and I do believe that your sister Belinda may well have fallen in love with him! Bless me, I really do!"

As Scrooge and Tiny Tim disappeared from view,

Creep came out of the dining-room and opened the library door.

"Luncheon—" Creep gave a loud hiccup and quickly placed his gloved hand over his mouth "—is served." Creep returned to the dining-room and held open the door.

"I have no intention," stormed Cratchit, as he and Mrs. Cratchit and Belinda proceeded towards their lunch, "of letting any young doctor mingle with my important guests! And that's final!"

"We'll see about that, sir!" retorted Mrs. Cratchit.

"Oh, Father," said Belinda tearfully, "he's such a charming young man."

"Final!"

Creep punctuated this with another violent hiccup. The trio trooped into the dining-room, and the old retainer followed, desperately chewing on one of his already badly chewed gloves.

An elderly horse, pulling a wobbling conveyance, turned into Mountjoy Square and made for Bob Cratchit's house on the southwest corner. Alas, the vehicle did not carry our hero, for Charles Dickens was at this particular moment still some twelve minutes away from the Cratchit residence, the hansom he had hired having just struggled up the slight slope to the top of St. Martin's Lane. The young author deeply regretted having given Hoskins, his driver, part of the day off for the purpose of acquiring grooming gifts for his two already well-pampered horses.

No, the conveyance creaking to a stop outside the Cratchits' door was, in fact, a trap, and it was driven by a decidedly ugly customer, Noel Axworthy, Master of Paradise Hall. He was in his fifties and was a big man and a small tyrant, the sort who bullies his inferiors and cringes to his superiors. He wore a rusty-black surtout with a threadbare velvet collar, a large hat, and shoes with extremely large buckles. He also had a coarse, leering voice to match his generally vile appearance.

A sign over one of the rickety trap's wobbly wheels bore a mud-stained legend that was virtually a contradiction in terms:

PARADISE HALL
Insured Against Accidents
—Funeral Parlour at Rear—

Axworthy climbed down and hammered on the door, which Creep, after a minute or three, duly opened.

"Axworthy, Paradise 'All. Sent for." Axworthy, who thought talking to servants a profligate waste of words, swept off his hat, revealing a mass of grey hair that was lank on the sides and matted on top and that, when last brushed and combed, looked as if it had received the tonsorial attentions of certain gardening implements.

Creep was nervous. "Oh, yes, sir. I'll fetch my master." He moved to take the visitor's hat, but Axworthy contemptuously waved him away, strode into the living-room, and surveyed the furnishings with his customary leer. Creep entered the dining-room and stayed there. After a moment Bob Cratchit came out.

"Ah, Axworthy," Cratchit began. "How went the hanging?"

Noel Axworthy, ever true to his evil nature, instantly became servile and made a feeble attempt at a joke. "Well, it went very well, I got there in the neck o' time, you might say. Trouble is, now I've three empty beds."

"Axworthy, I understand you have a new wing at Paradise Hall"—Axworthy nodded and twisted his hat in his hands—"and I have an elderly person I'd like to put in

58

your charge for a week or two. I want the best of care. Understand?"

"You can rely on Noel Axworthy, sir, I'll put that person in my finest suite, room one 'undred an' forty-eight."

"But I had no idea you had so many rooms!"

"Oh, I don't, sir," Axworthy explained obsequiously, "there's an 'undred an' forty-eight people livin' in the *one* room, if you understand my meanin'."

"No," said Cratchit impatiently, "what I want are private accommodations. I'm fully prepared to pay."

"Oh, it must be a relation." Axworthy fingered his chin. " 'Oo's the old lady, sir?"

"It isn't a lady." Cratchit became a little more impatient.

"Oh, it usually is, when an old 'un needs disposin' of." (For Axworthy, as you can imagine, was more than knowledgeable regarding such matters.) " 'Oo's the old gentleman, sir?"

"Mr. Ebenezer Scrooge."

Axworthy was completely bowled over. His eyes widened, his face cracked into an astonished smile, and he spread out his arms in wonderment: it is no exaggeration to say, therefore I'll say it, that Axworthy forgot himself to the extent that he almost didn't fawn on Bob Cratchit.

"Ebenezer *Scrooge?* Ebenezer *Scrooge?* 'E sent me all my best business! For years! Scores o' people—nay, 'undreds! One or two of 'em are still alive . . . I think. Well, this is most fittin', Mr. Cratchit, it'll be most appropriate to be able to welcome '*im.* 'E'll be the life an' soul of our little Christmas party."

Bob Cratchit went over to the sideboard where he stooped, opened the cupboard, and pulled out a green cloth bag tied with black twine. The contents clinked.

"Now I want him to get your most preferential treatment." Cratchit rose and turned again to Axworthy. "As I say, it's just for a week or two."

"Ah, they always say that, sir." Axworthy took the bag and weighed it in his shovel of a hand. " 'Eavy enough for a year or more. 'Ow much is in 'ere, guv'nor?"

"Twenty sovereigns in gold. He must have a private room! Your very best." (For, as we have said, Cratchit was quite naïve concerning the quality of the accommodations in such places.)

"Why, bless you!" exclaimed Axworthy gratefully, at the same time dropping his bag of new-found pelf into his upturned hat. "I can keep 'im till eighteen forty-seven on this!" His spiteful eyes narrowed, calling him to business. "Now, sir, where is 'e? Let's get 'im out o' the 'ouse!"

"No, he doesn't want to leave here until Boxing Day."

"That's another thing they always say, an' when it comes Boxin' Day, they say, 'Let's wait for the new year,' and when it comes New Year, they say, 'Let's wait for spring.' No, you take my tip, Mr. Cratchit, let 'im go while I'm 'ere. You can't trust the elderly. In any case, Mr. Scrooge'll understand; after all, in 'is day 'e made many others understand the same story—'ad to! An' when I tell 'im it's for a limited time only, just you watch 'ow 'is old face'll light up!" Axworthy wheezed hideously. "That was *'is* yarn!"

But Cratchit had moved away again, as people usually did when Axworthy breathed all over them during a long speech, except, of course, his inmates. Cratchit had opened Scrooge's door and looked in. He turned, puzzled to find the room empty.

"That's odd." Cratchit saw Creep emerge from the dining-room carrying a tray with nothing on it. "Creep! Where's Mr. Scrooge?"

"Oh, sir, he went upstairs with Master Tim," Creep answered truthfully, for he had indeed seen the two go up.

"Up—?" Cratchit was naturally surprised that Scrooge could negotiate the staircase, but Axworthy cut him off and addressed the butler.

"Well, you run up an' fetch 'im, ol' son."

Creep looked to Cratchit for confirmation, and, on receiving a brief nod, dutifully went upstairs.

"You leave this to me, Mr. Cratchit, sir," said Axworthy, "leave me in charge. You just go an' finish your lunch like the gentleman you are, sir."

Cratchit could think only of Lord Pouncey, Horace Huddleston, Sir Robert Peel, and his knighthood. So now, regrettably—and we must all, at times, have occasion to regret the traits and foibles of human nature, even, perhaps, our own—he lamely looked for an excuse to get away.

"He's upstairs, now, with my son, against my wishes! You see, Axworthy, how he meddles in my affairs?"

Axworthy strode purposefully into Scrooge's room. He feverishly opened drawers, throwing Scrooge's belongings into a large cloth bag he found. Cratchit looked around the doorway. "What are you doing, Axworthy?" he protested, though he knew very well. "I don't mean for you to take him yet! I only want you to put it to him."

"Oh, I'll put it to 'im, sir," said Axworthy, stuffing Scrooge's shirts and socks into the bag. "I'll put it to 'im in style!"

Cratchit heard footsteps coming downstairs. They belonged to Creep and Scrooge.

"Ah, Bob," Scrooge said, seeing Cratchit but not Axworthy. "I'm worried about Tiny Tim, you know, and I believe I know what's wrong with him. I believe it's because—"

"You can walk after all, then! Another deception!"

"No," said Scrooge, as Creep went into the dining-room, "as I was just telling Creep, a wonderful new medicine came to me this morning."

"So did something else," said Cratchit, indicating Scrooge's open door. "A friend."

"Oh? Of yours?"

"No. Of yours. He's come to take you away for a few days."

"No, Bob! Not before Christmas! Not before—"

Axworthy chuckled deeply on hearing this. He appeared in Scrooge's doorway, holding up Scrooge's night-shirt before ramming it into the bag. " 'Ullo, Mr. Scrooge. I'm just packin' yer nightie for ya."

Scrooge recognized the Master of Paradise Hall and was much frightened and alarmed. "Oh, no! Noel Axworthy! Don't tell me I have come to this!"

"It's only for a few days, Mr. Scrooge. Remember? An' now you'll be able to see for yourself 'ow some o' the unfortunates you've sent me 'ave 'ad to live. But you're lucky. Mr. Cratchit 'as kindly arranged for you to 'ave me best private quarters." Axworthy half-turned and reached up for something out of sight in Scrooge's room, groping high on the wall.

Scrooge succeeded in fighting back tears, but there's no denying that he was in great grief. Cratchit listened to the outburst that followed impassively; heard it, in fact, with equanimity.

"Merciful heaven, it's Providence revenging itself upon me!" Scrooge declaimed emotionally. "And I blame myself, I blame myself! I *deserve* to be taken, by you of all people, Axworthy, I who have sent you so many! Oh, yes! The greatest grief is the grief of retribution, retribution so well deserved! Oh, calamity! A calamity for me!"

If Cratchit had the impression that Scrooge possibly didn't care much for the idea of going, he kept quiet about it. Axworthy now produced Scrooge's hat and topcoat. "Now you just come an' put on yer 'at an' coat, ol' chap. We wouldn't want you to catch your death."

As Axworthy held up Scrooge's coat, the old man turned to Cratchit, his voice quavering. "Couldn't I, mayn't I, say good-bye to Tiny Tim? I beg of you!"

"Don't let 'im get round you, sir," Axworthy advised, helping poor old Scrooge into his coat. "Old folks is remarkably clever at whinin' and cringin'. Make the break clean an' sharp. An' wot's another Christmas? To 'im?"

Creep came out of the dining-room. "Excuse me, sir, but Mrs. Cratchit asks if you'll return to the luncheon-table."

Cratchit nodded curtly and turned back to Scrooge while Creep quietly tidied a few things on the sideboard. "You asked if it was important to me," he said determinedly. "Now you know how much. But I promise you will be back the first week in January, as soon as this business is over. You have my word." He took Scrooge's hand. "And thank you for your co-operation."

Cratchit marched to the dining-room door and opened it, but before he left the room, Scrooge called, "A merry Christmas, Bob! And a happy New Year, *Sir Robert!*"

Cratchit, stung, glowered in some surprise, then proceeded to the luncheon-table. Daisy came out with a tray piled with dishes.

"Sir Robert, eh?" Axworthy muttered. "I wondered wot'd changed 'im all of a sudden."

Creep plaintively addressed Scrooge, who was putting on an extremely long comforter. "Oh, sir, say it isn't happening. Say good-bye to Mr. Scrooge, Daisy, he's leaving us for a bit."

Daisy, her face clouding, set down the tray. "Oh, no, sir, no. We'll miss you. We'll all miss you."

"Look on the bright side, Daisy," said Scrooge, putting on his hat. "At least my gout has gone." He took two coins from his pocket and handed one to each servant. "Thank you both for your many services. And please take this. Each of you."

"Oh, thank you, sir!" But Creep and Daisy were very sad about taking anything from him.

Axworthy, who had the bag containing Scrooge's things in one hand and Cratchit's gold in the other, went out into the street and stood there, waiting. Daisy had become quite tearful, and Scrooge did his best to comfort her. "There, there, Daisy, at least there's one consolation. You'll have one less room to tidy."

Daisy replied with a barely stifled sob.

"And poor Tiny Tim," Scrooge went on as he approached the open front door, "that boy will be so lonely. Will you please go up to his room and give him a kiss and a cuddle from time to time?"

"Why, yes, sir," said Creep willingly, "I'll be glad to."

"Not *you*!" shouted Scrooge. "I mean Daisy!" But the old man was immediately contrite and placed his hand on Creep's arm. "I'm terribly sorry, please forgive me."

Axworthy called from outside the door. "Come on!"

Scrooge turned in the doorway. He was a decidedly sorry sight, his long comforter actually brushing the floor, and trying, as he was, not to weep. "Could someone tell my doctor where I am?" he asked Creep and Daisy. "Just in case ... And Mrs. Gubbins ... I should like that dear lady to know, too." He gave a drawn-out sigh as Creep and Daisy nodded vigorously. "Well, there's nothing more to be said."

"Yes, there is!" roared Axworthy from outside. " 'Urry up!"

It was then that Scrooge broke down, sobbing quietly in spite of himself. "Then may I wish you, Creep . . . and you, my dear Daisy . . . a very . . . merry . . . Christmas!"

The old man almost yelped the word "Christmas," for Axworthy's hand had fallen on his shoulder and yanked him out of the house. Creep very sadly closed the door.

"Is it possible," demanded Bob Cratchit, who had appeared in the dining-room doorway on the far side of the room, "that I might be able to get some service in here? Kindly shift yourselves! Make haste!"

Daisy, sniffing, and Creep, biting his lip, shifted themselves and made haste into the dining-room.

Tiny Tim, up in his room, was looking out of the window, his elbows resting on the window-ledge and his hands over his ears. He craned forward on seeing Scrooge and Axworthy leave the house and approach the decrepit horse and ramshackle trap he had been studying curiously.

Axworthy heaved himself into the driver's seat. The only other place for a passenger was on the bench next to him. After tossing Scrooge's belongings into a small space at the back and placing his bag of gold on his lap, Axworthy helped Scrooge up. Scrooge gasped and winced on sitting down: a small, bent nail had thrust its way through the seat, and Scrooge quickly rose, holding onto Axworthy for support. Axworthy grinned, threw Scrooge's bag on the seat for use as a cushion, and Scrooge sat down.

The old horse was given a couple of cracks, and the trap slowly pulled away, displaying yet another sign on the back. It read, and Noel Axworthy must surely have been one of the world's first hostelry-keepers to believe in the power of advertising, however misleading:

PARADISE HALL
Established 1798
". . . Where Inmates
Become Friends."

Down the street, a little way off, a street-musician continued to play "Joy to the World" on a penny-whistle, but Tiny Tim had stopped listening to him. He saw Scrooge lean back, just before turning the corner, and give a disconsolate little wave at the house, though to no one in particular.

The hansom-cab hired by Charles Dickens was now, it must be stated, exactly thirty seconds away.

Tiny Tim left his room and ventured part of the way downstairs. He saw Creep carrying a tray with coffee-cups on it towards the dining-room. "Oh, Creep! Mr. Creep!"

Creep stopped and looked up, his voice quavering. "Yes, Master Tim?"

"I was just looking out of my window, and I saw Uncle Scrooge!"

Creep now seemed on the verge of breaking down, for he said, pathetically, "Oh, please don't make me be the one to tell you, Master Tim! Don't let me be the one!"

Mrs. Cratchit came out of the dining-room. She was extremely puzzled and quite a bit worried. "Creep! What is happening? Daisy is sobbing all over the suet-pudding, and when I asked her what was wrong, my husband shushed her up."

"Oh, Mother," called Tiny Tim from halfway up the stairs. "Uncle Scrooge has just left, and with another man!"

"So!" Mrs. Cratchit was horrified to hear this.

"Before he went around the corner, he turned and waved at the house. But he didn't look up, Mother! He didn't look up!"

"We'll see about this!" Mrs. Cratchit strode grimly back into the dining-room. As the door closed behind her, the front door's knocker fell insistently upon its plate three times.

Creep put down his tray and waved Tiny Tim back upstairs. On opening the front door, he saw a youngish fellow with a door-knocker beard, a cape, a metal despatch-case, and a rather excited smile.

"Oh, I should like to see Mr. Scrooge, please," said the well-dressed gentleman politely. "And Mr. Cratchit."

"I'm afraid Mr. Scrooge isn't here, sir."

"Well, Mr. Cratchit, then." The gentleman stepped eagerly across the threshold, looking around him with interest.

"And who shall I say is calling, please, sir?" Creep enquired.

"My name is Dickens." The visitor removed his hat and handed it to Creep. "Charles Dickens," he added modestly. And the great author walked briskly into the living-room.

Creep did not react to the identity of the visitor, not yet, but merely closed the door and hung up his hat. Dickens meanwhile had gone over to the fireplace, where he looked up with a delighted smile at Scrooge's portrait. He then touched with a bemused look Tiny Tim's crutch, which, you will remember, was displayed beneath the painting, it being of no further use to the boy.

Almost wistfully—and Creep did not hear this— Dickens remarked, "Charming ... quite charming."

Creep came over, solicitously washing his hands with invisible soap. "May I take your cape, sir?"

Dickens said nothing: all he did was smile and shake his head, for he was still contentedly taking in the room.

"I'll tell Mr. Cratchit you are here, sir," Creep suggested. "He's just finishing his lunch."

"Oh, but I have no wish to disturb him." Dickens, impatient though he was, knew better than to drag a fellow Englishman away from the luncheon-trough.

"Well, may I offer you a sherry, sir, while you wait?"

Dickens nodded assent and continued to look around the room with delighted amusement.

"If I may be so bold, sir," ventured Creep, pouring the sherry, "wouldn't you be the young gentleman who began writing recently about the plight of London's poor?"

Dickens was always pleased when he was recognized, and he gave Creep a charming smile. "Couldn't have put it better myself. Yes, several years ago."

"Well, if I may respectfully say so—" Creep presented Dickens with his drink "—Cook downstairs has a copy of a book by you, sir. Oh, it's a great masterpiece."

"Really? Which one?" Amused, Dickens sipped his drink.

"It's a story we love below stairs." Creep smiled at the very thought of the book, and if he went on to sound vague, it must be remembered that Dickens, although well known at this particular time, was not, at the age of thirty-one, nearly as famous as he would become, nor were the titles of his works household words yet, with the exception of one of them, and as Creep now had difficulty recollecting even that one, it's not surprising that the young author found himself staring at his struggling admirer keenly, expectantly, and quizzically, all at the same time.

"It's about that portly gentleman," Creep continued, fingering a shiny blotch on his lapel—the remains of the

Hallowe'en pork—"who wanders through London getting up to all sorts of scrapes and hilarious adventures—oh, very droll, some of them are!"

The young author found himself fascinated. "He also went into the country, too," he said eagerly, not realizing he was guilty of perpetrating a grammatical redundancy, although Creep, it must be stated, did not notice it.

"Did he, sir? Oh, yes, that's right," Creep confirmed. "Now the jolly gentleman's name is Samuel ... er, it's on the tip of my tongue ... Samuel ... now what is it? Samuel ..."

Dickens could take no more. With a very slight note of irritation he asked quietly, "Would it, I wonder, be Pickwick?"

"That's him, sir!" Creep cried triumphantly as if he'd known it all along. "The very one! Good old Pickwick, sir!"

Dickens was greatly relieved. And now he heard an exchange, a heated argument, as Daisy came in from the dining-room, struggling in the doorway with a tray piled with dishes. What Dickens heard caused his eyebrows to shoot fully three-tenths of an inch above their normal position.

"I had no alternative, madam! You want to be a *lady*, don't you?"

"And I've a title for you, Bob Cratchit, an unpleasant title indeed!"

"Pray be silent, madam! I'll allow nothing whatever to interfere with my career! Do you understand me in this?"

"Only too well, sir! Only too well, I'm much afraid!"

Daisy closed the door, and as she crossed the living-room she saw and recognized Dickens. "Oh, excuse me, sir."

"Miss Wellbeloved, is it?" Dickens smiled and addressed the servant-girl gently and courteously, for he had a genuine compassion for all the lower orders. "I'm so pleased to see you again and do trust that you are well."

"Oh, thank you, Mr. Dickens, thank you, indeed."

Daisy, pleased and a little flustered at being greeted so politely, took her tray below stairs. Creep went into the dining-room with the coffee-cups, and again Dickens was surprised to hear a snatch of squabbling, the last thing he would have expected to hear in the Cratchit household on Christmas Eve.

"I am not prepared to listen to another word of argument!"

"Shame, Mr. Cratchit, sir! Shame! When it was Mr. Scrooge who saved you! Saved you, aye, and us!"

Luckily for Dickens the door closed behind Creep as he padded into the dining-room.

On their plodding progress to Paradise Hall, Scrooge and Axworthy proceeded down the Haymarket, awash with fruit and vegetable stalls offering, as was to be expected at this time of year, seasonal Christmas produce.

As the horse and trap passed the Hay Inn Axworthy grinned, transferred the reins to his other hand, and pulled a flask from his pocket. He took a generous swig and then, doubtless remembering Cratchit's injunction to take good care of Scrooge, offered the old man what remained in the flask.

Scrooge sadly shook his head. The horse and trap moved on down the Haymarket through happy crowds of Christmas shoppers, though Scrooge did not notice them.

Creep held the dining-room door open for his master and announced, "Mr. Dickens, sir."

Cratchit pulled his napkin from his throat, wiped his lips, and handed the napkin to Creep, who returned to the dining-room.

"Good day to you, sir." Cratchit looked rather curiously at his visitor. "How may I help you?" He added, quite unnecessarily, "Robert Cratchit."

Dickens came striding across the room, hand out-stretched, and shook hands eagerly. He spoke very rapidly and with great charm, gabbling so fast that Cratchit caught only a part of what he said and was not too interested, either, in what he did make out. As for the rest, it was jabberwocky.

"My dear Mr. Cratchit, sir, I feel I know you already! How is Mr. Scrooge, and Tiny Tim, and Mrs. Cratchit?" He took Cratchit's arm and steered him over to the fireplace, where they stood beneath the portrait of Scrooge.

"I've called because several months ago I had the very great pleasure of meeting Mr. Scrooge as he was being pushed in his chair in the Strand by your maid, and he was kind enough to invite me to join him in the forecourt of the Bank of Friendship ale-house, well, for an ale, and over it, Mr. Scrooge told me the remarkable and delightful story of the dream he had seven years ago that went on to change his life."

Cratchit stifled the beginnings of a yawn as Dickens raced on. "Well, sir, I was so struck by it, thought it all so heartwarming, that I've set it down as a Christmas story. It isn't much, it's a terribly slim volume, not much more than a pamphlet, really, but good enough, and perhaps cheap enough, to be plied by hawkers through the streets tomorrow and capture the Christmas Day reading trade—and, who knows? perhaps beyond—but my publishers, Chapman and Hall, standing by waiting for their presses to roll, they say to me, to *me*, mind: 'No!' They tell me they are becoming weary of the fanciful names I keep inventing!"

Only on hearing Dickens's next remark did Cratchit become slightly interested, as the young author warmed to his theme:

"For example, in the version my publishers have, Mr. Scrooge is called Gregory Flintlock. You, sir—forgive me—have become Algernon Muddlecombe. And Tiny Tim, to my publishers' everlasting regret, is now known as Lame Joe."

Cratchit now felt an uncontrollable urge to scratch himself on the behind, and he did, as he had become bored again. He also rubbed his right ankle with his left foot; and he made up his mind then and there to rebuke Creep for having admitted such a demented person to his home. But there was no stopping Dickens now.

"Now in view of my previous offerings—*Barnaby Rudge, Oliver Twist*, and *Martin Chuzzlewit*—actually, I'm still working on that last one now. Martin Chuzzlewit—ha! what a name—my publishers beg me to resort to less colourful names, and they suggest, why not, for a happy and innocuous story such as this, why not seek permission to use the actual names of the real and living characters? And I am beginning to be persuaded that the real names are much better!"

Dickens looked to Cratchit for an expression of interest, did not find one, so snapped open his metal despatch-case and pushed the first draft of his tale into Cratchit's unwilling hands.

"My title for it is, quite simply, 'A Christmas Carol', and here is a version in which the actual names are used. Will you kindly look at it, Mr. Cratchit, and give me your approval? You are mentioned early in the booklet, sir, and again, twice, very late, but hurry, if you will, for time is pressing. Well? How say you? How say you, sir? Well?"

And Dickens, panting, fell into a chair, snatched up his sherry-glass, and drained it gratefully.

Scrooge and Axworthy arrived outside Paradise Hall. Axworthy got down, carrying his bag of gold. Scrooge eased himself down to the street and took down the bag containing his belongings.

There was a colossal tearing sound as the sharp nail on the passenger's seat did its spiteful business, and Scrooge's shirts and socks fell upon the pavement. Scrooge looked down on them forlornly, then stooped to pick them up.

Creep opened the dining-room door and came into the living-room behind Mrs. Cratchit and Belinda. Bob Cratchit, who had reluctantly begun to glance at the manuscript, rose from his chair, and so, of course, did Dickens. But Cratchit immediately sat down again and resumed reading upon noticing that introductions weren't really necessary.

"Mr. Dickens, is it?" smiled Mrs. Cratchit, impressed at having such an important visitor and determined to put on a cheerful front despite her recent argument with her husband. "My butler was just telling me . . ."

"Mrs. Cratchit, ma'am?" Dickens bowed deeply. "It is an honour."

Mrs. Cratchit gushed, very brightly, "And this is my daughter, Belinda."

"Ah, Miss Cratchit," said Dickens, with a knowing twinkle. "Such a plucky girl."

Belinda gave a puzzled smile on hearing this but made no comment. Dickens went on, "And where is your little brother I have heard so much about? I would very much like to meet him."

"I'll run and fetch him, sir," said Belinda. "May I, Father?"

Bob Cratchit, now engrossed in the manuscript's first page, merely grunted. Belinda went upstairs.

"I've a copy of a book by you, Mr. Dickens," said Mrs. Cratchit, "and would be greatly obliged if you would do me the honour of signing the title-page."

"With the greatest of pleasure, madam," replied Dickens. "Which one is it?"

"Now what it's about is an old man and a little girl, and they run this funny shop just off the Kingsway."

Dickens's response was an expectant one; however, his voice rose before trailing off, as if he might be getting ready to face another disappointment, for all he said was, " Ye-e-e-e-s?"

"It's a charming little book," Mrs. Cratchit went on helpfully, "where they sell all sorts of knick-knacks and bric-a-brac. Now dearie me, whatever is that little shop called?"

"Would it be," Dickens suggested drily, *The Old Curiosity Shop?*"

"That's it, that's the one," Mrs. Cratchit acknowledged happily. "I'll go and fetch it."

The worthy matron hurried into the library as Belinda and Tiny Tim came downstairs.

"Sir, this is my brother Timothy." Belinda pushed the lad forward. "This is Mr. Dickens. He's an author."

"How do you do, sir," said Tiny Tim, shaking hands. "I'm sorry, but I haven't read anything you've written. Not yet."

"You don't know how pleased I am to hear that, Tiny

Tim," said the author with a slight and rueful smile. "But—oh, dear!—one can't refer to you as tiny! Not any more."

"Oh, that's all right, sir," said Tiny Tim politely. "Uncle Scrooge still calls me that."

"And where is the old gentleman?" asked Dickens.

"Well, er—"

"Here we are!" called Mrs. Cratchit, hurrying in from the library and carrying a book. "Here it is!"

Dickens went with her to a side-table and smiled as he reached for pen and ink. Mrs. Cratchit opened *The Old Curiosity Shop* at the title-page. Her husband looked up from his reading and gave an appreciative chuckle. "I really must say this is brilliant! You have captured old Scrooge magnificently!"

Dickens was naturally pleased to hear this.

Bob Cratchit chortled as he read from the manuscript: "'...tight-fisted hand at the grindstone ... squeezing, wrenching, grasping, scraping, clutching, covetous, old sinner'! I must and do commend you, sir! You truly have him!"

"Oh, yes," said Mrs. Cratchit as Dickens signed his name in her book, "but as he *was*. I do hope," she told Dickens concernedly, "you didn't write anything nasty about him."

Scrooge had picked up his belongings from the pavement and was entering the palatial front office of Paradise Hall. That hideous individual, Noel Axworthy, held the door invitingly open for him and called out to his even more hideous wife, perched behind her grille, "A new guest, my love!"

Scrooge glanced eagerly around at his new surroundings, though he wondered why the old biddy behind the counter was glaring at him. And why, Scrooge pondered, was she now snapping in his direction?

"Take off yer 'at!" was all she said. No word of welcome.

Scrooge struggled with his belongings as he did his best to oblige.

"Forgive 'er, Mr. Scrooge," said Axworthy by way of explanation. "My new bride o' three months." He handed his recent bride Cratchit's bag of gold, passing it through a gap in the grille. "Take this, Gloria," he commanded, "an' lock it in the safe. Mr. Scrooge is to 'ave our finest accommodations."

Gloria Axworthy's eyes flashed as she felt the weight of the bag, though she addressed Scrooge as sharply as before. "Leave yer 'at on!"

Scrooge stopped grappling with his things and gave Mrs. Axworthy a timid smile.

"Now wot's open, my love?" Noel Axworthy enquired of his unsightly spouse. "Private. Your very best. A suite."

Mrs. Axworthy gave Scrooge her imitation of a welcoming smile, then glanced at her registration-book. "I think I'll give 'im," she told her husband, "the Grey Room."

"Thank you, sir," said Mrs. Cratchit, happily applying a blotting-pad to Dickens's dedication. "I shall treasure this always."

No one noticed that Cratchit's smile had faded as he studied the manuscript, or that his eyebrows had met, or that he had started to glower. No one, not even the observant Dickens, who turned to Cratchit's son and enquired, "And what do you want to be when you grow up, Tiny Tim?"

A CALAMITY INDEED

"A doctor, I do believe, sir." The boy added, entirely without guile, for his ambition was sincerely held, "I should so like to help others."

"A doctor? Oh, yes!" Belinda Cratchit clasped her hands dreamily, though it must be admitted she was thinking of another. "I believe that to be wonderful!"

Behind them Bob Cratchit rose angrily, his face darkening in readiness for a storm. "I can't have this! I do not wish to be represented as a lowly clerk!" He threw the manuscript down onto the coffee-table. "You've made me out to be pathetic, Mr. Dickens, a naïve, unthinking simpleton!"

"Just as I remember you," cut in Mrs. Cratchit wistfully. "Lovable and sweet."

"I can assure you, Mr. Cratchit," Dickens assured his host, "that people will adore you."

"But they will not be the *right* people," Cratchit bristled. "Not necessarily!" He gave an irritable wave of his hand to the rest of his family. "Kindly leave us for a time. Mr. Dickens and I have business."

"Very well," said Mrs. Cratchit obediently, as was expected of a wife, at least when there was company. "Come, Belinda. We hope to see you again, Mr. Dickens."

"And me, sir!" called Tiny Tim, returning upstairs.

Dickens, glancing warily at Bob Cratchit's scowl, could only say he hoped so, too. Cratchit waited until his wife and daughter had gone down the corridor before giving vent to his thoughts.

"Your story, sir, if published, will ruin me! I'll be shunned by society; ridiculed, laughed at. Grovelling to old Scrooge, you have me—he's domineering over me! I'll not have it, sir! Publish, and I'll sue!"

"Oh, dear," said Dickens, who was beginning to regret his visit. "I wonder how Mr. Scrooge will react."

"What is the point, sir," Cratchit fumed, "in obtaining his permission and yet not attaining mine? I refuse to be made a laughing-stock!"

"But I am about to make you the most famous man in London!"

"The dickens you say!" Cratchit stormed, intending no pun, for the saying had been popular for centuries.

"Oh, but I do say," parried Dickens, drawing on his rapier-wit and smiling faintly in spite of the argument.

"I wish to be left alone! Fame is something I can achieve on my own. Why, a few days hence—" Cratchit hesitated, not wishing to reveal the news of his impending knighthood. "Kindly leave."

"May I not see Mr. Scrooge?" Dickens asked politely.

"You may not, sir!" The very mention of the old gentleman's name seemed to sting Cratchit, who abandoned caution and blurted: "He left this very day! For a hostelry in King William's Alley!"

Before Cratchit had time to regret having said this, he found himself in a nose-to-nose duel with the young author, who, although dangerously quiet, now had burning eyes. "You mean *Little* King William's Alley. You don't mean Paradise Hall?"

"I do! And I want no rumour or scandal! Not a breath!"

"The poor man. Did he go there of his own wish?" Dickens, receiving no reply, now went on intensely: "You talk to me of not a breath of scandal? This merely whets my appetite. I have had my share of unhappiness in my time and inform you, sir, that I shall proceed at once to Paradise Hall!"

But Cratchit had heard enough from his inquisitive visitor; he broke off the exchange and moved swiftly to the fireplace, causing Dickens to call after him, "If I can assist Mr. Scrooge, I shall!"

"You may proceed," said Cratchit, vigorously pulling the bell-rope and causing a bell to ring distantly below stairs, "where you like, sir. Good day!"

"And if any harm has befallen him," Dickens grated, "I shall communicate that fact to my former journalistic friends on the *Morning Chronicle*—aye, and the *Evening Chronicle*, where, it happens, they know me well!"

"Good day!" Cratchit's face twitched with rage as Creep came up to the living-room. "Creep, show this gentleman out."

Creep retrieved the visitor's hat and opened the front door. Dickens picked up his metal despatch-case and hurried towards the street.

Cratchit glanced down at the coffee-table—Dickens had forgotten his manuscript! Quivering with anger, Cratchit snatched up the first draft, with all its smudges and blots and alterations, and its soon-to-be-famous opening, "Marley was dead, to begin with." He turned to the fire and stooped, holding the pages over the flames. It is our good fortune that Dickens, now entering Mountjoy Square, remembered them.

Just as Creep was closing the door, Dickens strode back in, crossed the room at speed, and gently but firmly took the manuscript from Cratchit's hands, just in time. "I'll take that." The young author marched to the front door and said to himself, as Creep gaped and as Cratchit glared, "Phew! That was a near thing."

Now that he was sailing out through the door, Dickens became cheerful. " 'Twould have done you no good, Mr. Cratchit, sir," he called over his shoulder. "My publishers already have a second copy—with the *other* names. Good day to you! And watch for the *Chronicle*'s final edition!"

On this ominous note, which made Cratchit grimace—for the last thing he wanted was adverse publicity—

Dickens threw a quick and knowing smile at Creep, tugged down the brim of his hat determinedly, and stepped out into the square. This time he found a hansom at once, for Mountjoy Square was blessed with a cab-rank on the south side.

"Where to, guv?" asked the driver, picking up the reins.

On giving his instructions, even Dickens eschewed his usual flowery circumlocution, for all he said was, "Little King William's Alley. Paradise Hall."

Charles Dickens intended to keep his promise. He would, he had nobly decided, go to the aid of poor old Ebenezer Scrooge, give him comfort, and if necessary rescue him.

If anyone had had the temerity to inform the young author that Scrooge did not require his assistance, would be sorry even to see him, and would soon be fervently wishing that his visitor would go away, then I am afraid that Dickens, in all his righteous indignation and for all his humanity and social conscience, would have dismissed such a person as being quite mad—indeed, would have accused him of it.

The cab moved off.

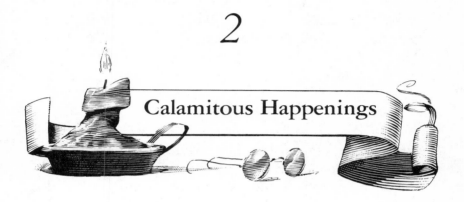

2

Calamitous Happenings

Scrooge's face fell, like the faces of countless others before him, as soon as he went from the imposing and misleading reception-area into the gloomy labyrinth of Paradise Hall.

Still carrying his belongings, and accompanied by Noel Axworthy, Scrooge trudged up dimly lit and treacherous stone steps and entered a dank and drab corridor with several locked and bolted doors leading off from it.

On reaching the first of these doors, Axworthy rapped on it and paused. A man on the other side promptly coughed; Axworthy smiled and moved on. He tapped on the second door, and a woman behind it cleared her throat loudly, whereupon Axworthy gave a nod of satisfaction and marched to the third door, behind which, on hearing a knock, the man inside had a coughing-fit.

It was not without a shudder that Scrooge realized that Axworthy was ascertaining whether the respective inmates were alive or dead.

But when Axworthy tapped on the fourth door:

silence. He listened intently, frowned, then cupped a hand around his mouth and shouted a command to an assistant who must have been lurking in the shadows way back down the corridor.

"Check Number Four!" The Master of Paradise Hall then addressed Scrooge confidentially, though it was clear that Axworthy didn't really care about the fate of Number Four's inhabitant. " 'E didn't answer me yesterday, either."

Scrooge and Axworthy moved on and passed through a doorway.

The Grey Room proved to be just as its name suggested: grey walls, a grey floor, and, to complete the effect, a ceiling to match. The room was small but clean. Scrooge placed his shirts and socks and odds and ends on the table and took in the room's other furnishings: a bed with an iron bedrail, a bedside-table, a chair, a stool, and a window covered, for obvious reasons, with stout iron lattice-work through which streamed the afternoon sun.

" 'Ere we are, Mr. Scrooge," said Axworthy, looking about the room proudly and remembering Cratchit's orders to him to take good care of the old man. "The finest quarters in the buildin', after mine. I was told to give you me most careful treatment, so this 'as been reserved for you especially."

"Spacious!" exclaimed Scrooge, looking around the tiny room. "It's positively spacious, after my little cloakroom. But—" he pointed with some consternation to the door-way "—where's the door? Where on earth is the door?"

"Door?" echoed Axworthy. "Oh, there isn't one. What d'you want a door for?"

Scrooge looked at him blankly. "But how can private living-quarters not yet possess a door?"

"Wot do you expect 'ere?" Axworthy shrugged. "Buckin'am Palace? You're lucky there's no door; it cuts down on draughts. Cruel things, draughts is. It's the chill that kills, especially 'ere."

Scrooge took off his hat, topcoat, and long comforter and hung them on a couple of wall-pegs. "Why," he asked, "was there such formality downstairs to enter your establishment?"

"Oh, that isn't the 'alf of it, Mr. Scrooge," Axworthy explained deferentially, "you try gettin' out." He indicated the bedside-table. "Now you'll note, sir, there's an 'andbell on your little bedside-table that you can ring for service at any hour o' the day or night."

"A handbell . . . that's extremely thoughtful of you."

"Yeah," said Axworthy, who was pleased that Scrooge was pleased. "Just give it a dingle, an' you'll find yer every whim will get our swift an' prompt attention. From expert staff. You'll find that service 'ere, sir, is a practised art."

"I'll try it." Scrooge picked up the handbell and duly dingled.

The wheedling, reedy voice of an approaching woman came immediately from the corridor. "Ye-e-s? Ye-e-s? Tessie's comin', Tessie's 'ere."

Through the gloom came a woman dressed in rags. Her face was dirty, her hair was all over the place, and several of her teeth were missing. Her appearance made her age impossible to determine, but from her manner it soon became apparent that she was a kind, if simple, soul. "Merry Christmas," she said pleasantly, "a very merry—"

"Clear off, y'ol' biddy!" Axworthy roared this out with startling ferocity. "Sling yer 'ook! This was only a test!"

"Oh, sir," said Scrooge as the woman cowered and backed away, "may I not return her most cordial greeting?" He smiled at her and bowed. "And a merry Christmas to you, madam, a merry Christmas indeed!"

The woman grinned and shambled forward, making

Axworthy feel it incumbent upon him to effect introductions. " 'Er name's Tessie Witherspoon. She's our oldest survivin' inmate."

Scrooge didn't mean to sound rude or inquisitive; he was merely interested. "How old is she?" he asked.

"Twenty-seven," Axworthy replied. "Now if, in the evenin's, you feel a trifle chilly in yer bed, just ring yer little 'andbell an' Tessie will fetch you a sizzlin' warmin'-pan, a burnin' 'ot toddy, an' she'll tell you a few stories to send you to sleep." Axworthy chuckled as though he remembered some of Tessie's best anecdotes, then addressed her firmly. "Now shove 'orf an' make yer rounds. Tell me 'oo's died this afternoon."

"Permission to speak, sir?" Tessie pleaded. "Please grant me your permission."

"All right. I feel generous."

Tessie grinned and threw a proprietorial nod in Scrooge's direction. "I like him," she admitted. "I quite, quite like him." She shuffled off down the corridor as Scrooge sat down on the bed and began to take off his boots.

"You see 'ow popular you're becomin' already, Mr. Scrooge?" Axworthy enquired patronizingly.

"Oh, the poor woman. Why was she sent here?"

Axworthy clasped his hands behind his back and took long paces, each of which tended to punctuate his reply. "She wasn't *sent* 'ere, guv, she was *born* 'ere. 'Er parents owed me *money* they could never *pay*, an' after they was 'anged, I *kept* 'er, right from a *baby*." Axworthy stopped pacing and reflected, "She's never yet set foot out o' Paradise 'All . . . Never will."

"Ah," said Scrooge, raising one of the boots he had removed and disconsolately staring at it, "the fate of so many unfortunates! A hard and brutal life of deprivation and squalor!" Almost absent-mindedly, he tossed the boot into a corner where it caused a tremendous clatter and injured a dozing mouse. "And in such a tawdry and terrible place!"

Axworthy, who was not listening—or was pretending not to—looked thoughtfully around the room as Scrooge untied his other boot.

"Wot this room needs, y'know, is a little bit o' brightenin' up. The festive air." He strode to the doorway. "I know the very thing, the very decoration to make your old face sparkle. Back in a minute. This room will be transmogrified before yer very eyes!"

Axworthy went eagerly down the corridor. Scrooge held up his remaining boot, and, being alone, he spoke to it. "Ah, the agony! O cruel and fickle Fate! And my feet are killing me again!" He hurled the boot with quite some force into another corner. "And I believe I forgot that new potion for my gout! Oh, where's my potion?"

Scrooge's potion was at that moment in a brown paper-bag being carried by Creep, who was sneaking up the outside basement steps into Mountjoy Square looking worried and furtive, having left the Cratchit residence without permission.

Fonsdale, Bob Cratchit's driver, had put the family horse and carriage in the little mews adjoining. Creep walked into the mews virtually on tiptoe, climbed up into the driver's seat, and reached, somewhat nervously, for the reins. At this moment Hercules, Bob Cratchit's horse, turned his head and threw the upstart driver a malevolent look. Hercules nodded sagely, for he had the distinct impression that here was a butler who had never driven a rocking-horse, let alone a full-blown horse and carriage: Hercules now knew exactly what to do.

Just as Cratchit's horse was drawing this conclusion Fonsdale, unseen by Creep, was on his hands and knees in the lane at the back of the carriage chewing on a wad of tobacco and polishing, with the aid of a spit and a rub, a small or imagined scratch.

Hercules bolted.

Eustace Fonsdale, to give Cratchit's driver his full and proper name—though that *still* is not correct, for his full name was Eustace Cedric Wilberforce Fonsdale—blew a bubble of disbelief on finding himself rubbing the empty air. He rose in bewilderment and, not caring a fig about the manure that Hercules had deposited, ran forward, slipped, and fell. As he sat at the top of the mews chewing on his tobacco, Fonsdale wondered why anyone would commandeer his master's horse and carriage and, finding no solution to the conundrum, rose and slipped and fell again.

Bob Cratchit, wearing the new top-hat he had bought himself for Christmas—primrose yellow, purple band—opened the front door, stepped out, pulled on his gloves, and stared in the direction taken by Creep or, rather, by the horse.

Cratchit had emerged from the house fully intending to avail himself of the services of his horse, carriage, and driver and was just in time to see the carriage career around the corner and head in the general direction of Hyde Park. He glanced down at his squatting driver, moved to assist him, thought better of it, and strode angrily off.

The front door opened again, and this time Belinda and Tiny Tim, both carrying packages wrapped in Christmas paper, came out; like Creep, the two looked furtive. They looked in the direction taken by their father, then made off, hoping to find a cab.

Fonsdale, on seeing Miss Belinda, struggled to his feet, gave a self-conscious smile, raised his hat, and slipped and fell again.

Scrooge, now bootless, hung his jacket on a wall-peg and had what he considered a brilliant idea: he clasped his hands, half-closed his eyes, and spoke directly, almost pleadingly, to the Grey Room's murky ceiling. "Jacob Marley ... Jacob Marley ... Come to me now, Jacob, and tell me why I do deserve this ... I'm imploring you, beseeching you, let me hear those clanking chains!"

To Scrooge's delight, he at once heard several clanking sounds. Encouraged by this, he looked expectantly about the room. "I hear you, Jacob! Come to me! I don't mind which wall!"

An awful, old bearded Figure in a cloak emerged from the gloom and stood in the doorway. Scrooge fell to his knees before him. "Oh, Jacob, I knew you would not fail me! My dear old partner and friend! How are you and the others? Tell me they are all well!"

The Figure boomed and clanked in the most terrifying fashion. "What," the Figure demanded, "do you know of me?"

"I know one thing!" Scrooge answered, and not without a pang of disappointment. "I can't see through you!"

"You cannot see through me?" The Figure was puzzled to learn that he was not at all transparent.

"And where are your chains? The ones you had to walk about the earth with? You're supposed to be girdling the globe with a penalty!"

The Figure pulled a rope tied around his waist, and a

"Wait!" Scrooge shouted in disbelief. *"I do believe I know that
awful face! Those vacant eyes, that dagger-like nose!"*

huge bunch of heavy keys came into view. Scrooge rose from the floor and peered at the unattractive countenance of his most unghostly visitor. "Wait!" he shouted in disbelief. "I do believe I know that awful face! Those vacant eyes, that dagger-like nose!" He jabbed his finger at the nose's point. "You're Zachary Makepeace, Zachary Makepeace, one of the ones *I* sent here! It's me, Scrooge, don't you know me?"

Zachary Makepeace made no direct reply. Instead he clasped his hands, closed his eyes—but not before the faintest trace of a wild light had appeared in them—and fervently began to talk to the ceiling, just as Scrooge had done. Makepeace, however, appeared to be devoutly and piously addressing not one but several beings in the far reaches of space who were, he was convinced, extremely interested in his tirade, which, while it continued, caused Scrooge to lick his lips with growing apprehension.

"Thanks to Saint Joan," Makepeace began, "Saint Jude, and all the other blessed saints. This will be advertised, as I solemnly pledged, in the *Evening Chronicle* and the *Westminster Gazette*, so that the world may know my prayers have been answered, and that this rapacious, ranting, and cantankerous old moneybags—I might almost say 'ratbag'—has been duly delivered into my hands. Thanks also to Saint Enoch of Constantinople and Saint Birtwhistle of Belgrade. For *thirty years* I have waited. At times I thought you would not heed me, and for this flagrant lack of faith I truly beg forgiveness."

"How are you keeping, Zachary?" Scrooge asked.

Makepeace opened his eyes and began to twist his hands menacingly. "You sold me up in eighteen-twelve! Sent me here, had me confined! And I only owed you five pounds ten!"

"D'you know," remarked Scrooge pleasantly, "I was

looking it up the other day, and d'you know that now, with interest, you owe a hundred and thirty-seven thousand pounds, sixteen shillings, and sixpence?"

Makepeace's eyes bulged at the very mention of such an amount: it was incredible that he could possibly owe old Scrooge so much. Scrooge glanced down at Makepeace's twitching hands and did his best to reassure their brooding owner; a magnanimous gesture of some sort now seemed to be in order.

"But I am not *counting*, Zachary," Scrooge said soothingly, "and to bring you peace of mind, I now forgive the debt. And I confidently anticipate that with your known generosity of spirit, you will forgive my little oversight in despatching you to this dreadful establishment some thirty-odd years ago. How the time flies! I forgot all about you! It's as simple as that."

The hands of Zachary Makepeace fluttered up, but Scrooge was saved by the return of the Master of Paradise Hall, who marched in carrying a jam-jar in which reposed two pathetic sprigs of holly and mistletoe. "'Olly an' mistletoe, comin' right up!" Axworthy announced. "Just wot this place needs."

Only now did Scrooge reveal his nervousness, running behind Axworthy and shouting, "He's going to kill me! He fully intends that I shall be deceased!"

"Wot are you doin' in 'ere?" Axworthy asked Makepeace in a most unpleasant tone. "Now you just leave Mr. Scrooge alone. 'Arm one 'air of 'is 'ead, an' I'll take them keys away from yer."

Makepeace instantly became servile. "Forgive me, Master." He backed away and bowed. "Just paying my respects."

"Get out," said Axworthy.

"Yes, at once. I humbly crave and beg your pardon." Makepeace actually went out backwards. "Good day, Mr. Scrooge, and welcome to our home." With a sly and sinister smile the turnkey traipsed back into the corridor's gloom.

"I'd be a bit wary of 'im if I was you, Mr. Scrooge." Axworthy placed the jam-jar on the table thoughtfully. " 'E killed a man 'ere once. Strangled 'im. Powerful 'ands! Like an ape or g'rilla. I got 'im orf, said it was self-defence. But them 'ands! Them terrible 'ands!"

"And them keys," said Scrooge, sitting on the bed and unbuttoning his shirt-collar, "those keys—why does he have so many?"

" 'E's turnkey now for the upper floors, wherever people is locked. But there's one key Makepeace'll never 'ave: the one to the front door."

Scrooge swung up his feet, placed his head on the pillow, and reclined on the bed at his ease. "Oh, such misery," the old gentleman declaimed, "the abject misery of it all!" He closed his eyes and reflected that the outlook was indeed as black as he had thought. "I feel so weary, I think I'll have a little nap. Would that I should never wake up!"

"Don't say that, Mr. Scrooge," said Axworthy with genuine concern, "for if you're dead, I'm done for. Bob Cratchit won't pay any more rent. An' I expect more if 'e gets a knight'ood."

Axworthy picked up the Grey Room's neatly folded grey counterpane and began to cover the old man.

Downstairs, in the Paradise Hall reception-area, Mrs. Axworthy poured herself a glass of gooseberry wine and squinted warily through the grille: a young man with a door-knocker beard and a deep frown had come in, his cape billowing behind him, and carrying a metal despatch-case.

"Mr. Scrooge, please."

Mrs. Axworthy gave him a little grin of recognition, for the gentleman had visited her establishment several times before during the furtherance of his career as an author.

" 'Ell-lo, love," she said. "if it isn't young Mr. Dixon." (This was a deliberate mistake on her part.)

"I wish to see Mr. Scrooge," said Dickens irritably.

"Sorry, pet, 'e's not to be disturbed." Mrs. Axworthy sipped her wine. " 'E's upstairs resting."

Indignant, Dickens pulled out an official-looking document from somewhere under his cape and waved it in the termagant's face. "Now look here! I have the authority, issued to me by the Bow Street magistrates—"

"I *know*," said Gloria Axworthy sweetly, even a shade flirtatiously, "it's to 'elp you with your scribblin', isn't it, love? You oughta be careful wot you write, dear," she told England's great social reformer. "You'll give this place a bad name."

For a reason best known to himself, Dickens began to bellow. "I have the authority to enter and inspect all establishments of low repute such as this and, if necessary, the right to expose you, madam!"

"That'll be nice."

"Aye, and your vile and evil-smelling husband!"

"Oo, fancy. 'Im, too, eh?" Her eyes narrowed, and she leaned forward confidentially. "Tell me, Mr. Dickinson, 'ave you never 'ad in yer life a bloomin' unspoken thought?"

Dickens, it must be admitted, was momentarily nonplussed. "Well, no," he began, "as a matter of fact, as a writer, I can't say I . . . I demand to see Mr. Scrooge!"

Mrs. Axworthy smiled one of her ghastliest smiles, looked down, and consulted her register.

"Now you toddle orf into dreamland," Axworthy advised Scrooge, having tucked him in under the counterpane, "an' I'll tell the choir not to re'earse their Christmas carols till you've slept."

The news that Paradise Hall was blessed with a choir caused Scrooge to open his eyes, but he accepted the fact of its existence and said nothing.

"You do like the 'olly, don't you, sir?" Axworthy went on, indicating the jam-jar on the table. "It really brightens the place with that jovial Christmas feelin'."

Scrooge turned his head on the pillow and stared at the jar, generously conceding that the Grey Room's ambience had been dramatically improved. "Ah, those brave little berries! Those plucky little leaves!" he exclaimed. "Would that Christmas lasted the whole year through!"

"The merry faces of the children . . ." Axworthy now became sentimental; he had not had time to have any. "The 'appy shouts an' laughter of the stupid little perishers . . ."

"Are there any children here at Paradise Hall?" Scrooge asked wistfully.

"No."

"Thank God . . . Oh, no! I'm slipping into my old habits; it must be these bleak surroundings. It's a tendency I shall have to resist." Scrooge had raised his head, but now rested it again. "But I do fear I am actually beginning to like it here . . . It's so quiet . . . so peaceful."

The Paradise Hall choir, assembled somewhere in the lower regions of the building, chose this moment to begin to sing "God rest ye merry, gentlemen, let nothing you dismay."

Axworthy, incensed, strode to the doorway and shouted down the corridor, "Shut up! Mr. Scrooge is 'avin' forty winks! Don't start again till I tell yer!"

The singing stopped. Scrooge placed his hands over his ears, Axworthy's stentorian commands having irritated them. "Oh, my head! Could I possibly have a headache powder?"

"Now wot do you want an 'eadache powder for," Axworthy chuckled insolently, "when you've already *got* an 'eadache?" He softened on seeing Scrooge twitch, went to the bedside-table, and picked up the handbell. "Oh, all right. Now you watch this for service."

Upon hearing the bell, Tessie Witherspoon came rushing through the doorway at once. "Tessie's here! Need a warming-pan?"

"Shut yer 'ole!" Axworthy roared, causing Scrooge to wince again. " 'Old 'ard! All 'e wants is an 'eadache powder. Fetch 'im yer strongest draught."

Axworthy gripped Tessie's shoulders, spun her around, and sent her scurrying out. Scrooge, panting on his pillow, was now, the poor old gentleman, thoroughly fed up.

Hercules, Bob Cratchit's horse, had first taken Creep to Mrs. Henrietta Gubbins's house in Mincing Lane, stopping only because of the crowded street, and he now paused outside the premises of the Cratchit family's doctor in Bonemarrow Drive. Hercules had condescended to stop a second time because Creep had made a shouted promise that he would give him his feedbag; that feedbag was now empty, Hercules noted, and Creep was still in the doctor's house.

CALAMITOUS HAPPENINGS

A sign on the wall adjoining the door read:

Dr. LORNE LOVEJOY
—Family Doctor—
POX CLINIC ON PREMISES

and, beneath it, a new name-plate had been tacked on:

& ERASMUS YOUNGBLOOD, M.D.

Hercules, munching on nothing, saw the front door open and Creep come out with Dr. Youngblood, who carried his shiny new doctor's bag. Youngblood tapped himself on the head, having forgotten his hat, and went back inside.

Creep climbed up into the driver's seat, and Hercules, far from satisfied with the taste of the feedbag's canvas, threw the butler a decidedly dirty look. After a moment Dr. Youngblood came out of the house, put on his hat, and stared as if he were delivering triplets.

Both Creep and Hercules were gone.

Tessie Witherspoon, the oldest surviving inmate of Paradise Hall, sat on the edge of an old tin bath in the high-walled yard at the back of the premises. Someone had long ago chalked "XXX" on the bath's side. Swishing a long stick with a metal cup attached to it in the bath's contents, Tessie poured the liquid she obtained into a glass, took a quick sip, and was satisfied that the mixture was good. She picked up from her lap a twist of paper containing headache powder, tossed the stick and its cup back into the bath, and hurried into the dingy rear part of the building, singing, as she did, a ditty.

The choir's conductor, out for a breather, at once told her to be quiet, then went to the bath himself.

Zachary Makepeace, that most unfriendly turnkey, encountered Dickens on the landing, took him to Scrooge's room, then slunk away.

Noel Axworthy, about to leave the Grey Room so that Scrooge could sleep, greeted Dickens with as little cordiality as he could muster. "Oh, no! Wot did the stupid woman let *you* in for? Another trouble-maker. Always was."

Dickens ignored him, strode eagerly over to Scrooge, and grasped the tired old gentleman's hand. "My dear Mr. Scrooge, I came at once when I heard of your predicament. How are you, sir? Are you well?"

Scrooge was perplexed. Try as he might, he simply could not put a name to the face of his visitor, though niggling at the back of his mind was a vague recollection of having seen this young fellow somewhere before. If Dickens had but mentioned the Bank of Friendship alehouse and their long chat in its forecourt several months before, and had he reminded Scrooge of his dream concerning Marley and his attendant ghosts, then Scrooge would have recalled the identity of his visitor instantly; but Dickens did not, and Scrooge, being rather old, had quite forgotten about it and about him. Such, I am afraid, is life.

"I said," Dickens pressed, "are you well?"

"Well," said Scrooge faintly, wondering who the devil this was, "I was resting until . . ."

" 'Oo invited you?" shouted Axworthy, feeling that the bedside conversation had gone on long enough. "This is a *private* 'ome!"

"And this establishment, sir," retorted Dickens, "is a

private disaster-area where tragically, under the law, you are permitted to conduct your reprehensible operations and your dastardly vendettas! But I have the right to enter here!"

"I've 'eard this before, so stop natterin'."

"Clear out!" thundered Dickens.

"Oh, my head," moaned Scrooge.

"Always meddlin' in events that don't concern yer! Inventin' a pack o' lies!" Axworthy stamped to the doorway, then turned and addressed the squirming Scrooge. "Soon as 'e's outstayed 'is welcome, ring yer 'andbell, an' I'll throw the 'ypocrite out." He fired a parting shot at the young author. "The poor man's friend, yet dresses like a dandy; likes to visit the work'ouse, yet lives in a bloomin' great mansion. Ha!"

Axworthy stormed out and narrowly missed colliding with Tessie Witherspoon, who hurried in to Scrooge and gave him the full glass and the headache powder.

Dickens did not notice Tessie's arrival, for he had begun pacing and studying the floor. To Scrooge's irritation, Dickens began to jabber, giving vent to the burning topic in which his brilliant mind was now engrossed. "What I desire to know, sir, is, were you conveyed here of your own volition, or were you transported unwillingly, as it were, carried, dragged, or by any other means against your will?"

"It doesn't matter very much," Scrooge murmured, untying the twist of powder. "I don't think I really mind."

"I knew it!" Dickens exclaimed. "I tell you, this Bob Cratchit must be exposed! Consigning *you* here, you of all people, the very man who changed his—"

Dickens broke off: he had looked up and seen Tessie, her mouth resembling a checkerboard as she smiled admiringly at Scrooge.

"What in—?" Dickens checked himself, not wishing to sound impolite. "Don't tell me this is your nurse?!"

"Her name," Scrooge told him, "is Tessie Witherspoon."

Dickens was electrified. "What a name!" He resumed pacing, studying his shoes. "I really must remember that. Oh, no—my publishers! Perhaps I had better try to forget that I have ever heard it."

Scrooge took advantage of Dickens's distraction to clutch Tessie's arm and whisper urgently, "Who *is* that fellow?"

" 'E's been 'ere before, guv," Tessie whispered back, her simple soul delighted to be of service. "Name o' Dickens . . . I believe 'e's a singer."

"Oh, no!" Scrooge cried, having taken the headache powder and gulped from the glass. "I can't stand it! My throat!"

Tessie touched his forehead with concern. "Wotever is the matter, guv'nor?"

"It's gin!" Scrooge gasped. "Pure, unadulterated gin!"

"Yes, it *is* adulterated!" Tessie placed the unfinished glass on the bedside-table, rose, and moved spiritedly to the doorway to resume her duties elsewhere. "That's the best gin in London; we got a bathful of it downstairs. It's called 'The Pride o' Chapel Street Market'. You won't 'ave an 'eadache after *that*. See you in a moment. Yer next course is lunch."

When Tessie had gone, Dickens gripped his chin while Scrooge nursed his painful throat. "Not, my dear friend, that I wish to extract with undue relish any of the drama of the situation in which you find yourself, for even my imagination has been quite plundered of late, and yet I am determined to bring this unco-operative fellow, Cratchit, to book. I intend to fetch a journalist-friend to interview you!"

An awful light of recognition dawned on Scrooge's face; he passed a trembling hand over his eyes. "Oh! *Now* I remember you!"

Dickens plunged on. "Did I tell you that I have set down the story you told to me? It took me a terribly long time, three and a half weeks, but I cherish the hope that long after my hand is as withered as the pens it held, my little pamphlet will be found on many a dusty bookshelf and with many a better book. I am proud of it! As I am proud indeed, my dear Mr. Scrooge, of you!"

"Really." Scrooge said this drily and entirely without interest; hoping that Dickens would go away, he pulled up the counterpane, covering his head. Dickens, meanwhile, was pacing swiftly and glancing down like a Buckingham Palace sentry with a pair of ill-fitting trousers.

"And in the writing of 'A Christmas Carol', I was like a child for there seems to me a magic in the very *name* of Christmas! And as I wrote about you, and in the intervals when I walked the streets of London by night, pausing in some of the inns and ale-houses that abound, I launched into dithyrambs of unbridled avidity concerning the wonderful tale you had told me, and revelling in it, aye, to anyone and everyone who might care to listen, and, as I did, laughing and weeping, my friend, both at the same time, for is it not, and I put this to you, the most compelling story?"

Dickens stopped pacing, looked to the bed for an answer, and was surprised to see that Scrooge was now completely covered. He went over to the bed and, still holding his despatch-case, stood poring over Scrooge.

It was at this moment that Mrs. Gubbins, Scrooge's

former housekeeper, appeared in the doorway carrying a steaming canister. She was accompanied by Zachary Makepeace, who pointed grimly to the bed, then clanked away.

"Oh, Doctor!" cried Mrs. Gubbins, drawing the worst conclusion on seeing Scrooge covered up. "Then I'm too late, too late! Wot time did 'e die, Doctor? I 'ad a terrible spasm in me left elbow at a quarter past two, so I knew someone close to me 'ad gorn. Oh, no! Now I'll 'ave to 'ave a seance for 'im!"

Dickens turned and gazed at her as she brokenly addressed what she believed to be Scrooge's corpse.

"Don't you worry, I'll bring you back. 'Enrietta Gubbins will 'ave you back in a jiffy!" She offered her steaming canister to Dickens. "Will you drink up the soup I brought for 'im, Doctor? Will you partake of 'is soup?"

Scrooge pulled back the counterpane and sat up. "Soup?" he asked eagerly. "What soup?"

"Oh, Mr. Scrooge!" Mrs. Gubbins fell with relief into a chair by the bed. "For a moment I thought we'd lost you! Dear me! Drink up this soup, you dear ol' darlin'. It was Creep, the butler, 'oo told me you was 'ere. 'E didn't give me a lift 'ere, though."

Scrooge opened the bedside-table's drawer and took out a spoon. "This is Mr. Dickens; Mrs. Gubbins is my former housekeeper."

Dickens, who had returned to his pacing-place, permitted his jaw to drop. "You don't mean the lady who nearly sold your bed-curtains?"

"I never," said Mrs. Gubbins indignantly, "did no such thing!"

She unscrewed the top from the canister, sending a cloud of steam into Scrooge's expectant face. Dickens resumed his sentry duty.

"Do you know, Mrs. Gubbins, the most astonishing thing? In my little booklet I mention Mrs. Dilber, the laundress—"

" 'Ow d'you know about 'er?" Mrs. Gubbins asked as Scrooge wiped his steaming eyes. "Died years ago, poor thing."

"And Old Joe," said Dickens, executing a neat about-turn, "I have him, the receiver of stolen goods—"

"Went for a walk in the Thames last Febrooary. Drowned 'imself."

"Oh!" Scrooge had helped himself to a spoonful of soup, and he now let out a wail. "This is terrible! It's nothing but scalding alcohol!"

"You ladle that down yer innards. That's boilin' 'ot rum, with a beef-cube in it."

"Oh, but I can't, I can't!"

"Drink it! 'Enrietta Gubbins knows wot's good for you."

Scrooge muttered something under his breath and obeyed reluctantly and with much distaste. But his old eyes positively widened in horror when he heard Mrs. Gubbins's next remark.

"And when you've drunk it," the good lady told him, "you're comin' 'ome with me."

Mrs. Axworthy, her pen poised over her register, scowled as Tiny Tim and Belinda, still carrying their Christmas packages, entered the reception-area. Tiny Tim, of course, was the perfect little gentleman.

"Good afternoon, madam. We've brought some Christmas presents. For Uncle Scrooge."

" 'Ow do I know 'e's yer uncle?"

"Well, as a matter of fact, he isn't, madam," answered Tiny Tim truthfully. "We just call him that."

Mrs. Axworthy reached greedily through the gap in the grille. "In that case you can't see 'im, then. You just give them things 'ere to me. I'll see 'e gets 'em. Eventually."

"Oh, but you don't understand. My name is Cratchit, and this is my sister."

A man's voice suddenly came from the far side of one of the reception-area's gold-painted pillars. The voice was that of Noel Axworthy, the Master, who had been standing, leaning against the pillar with his arms folded, unseen by the young visitors. Upon hearing that they were members of the family he now sought to serve, all things became possible.

"It's all right, Gloria," Axworthy commanded gruffly. "Let 'em through."

Scrooge now appreciated the flavour of Mrs. Gubbins's soup so well that he had dispensed with the spoon and, holding the canister with both hands, was drinking straight from it.

Mrs. Gubbins's eyes were swivelling back and forth like an umpire's at a tennis match, following Dickens as he walked and talked.

"Actually, I should quite prefer him to remain where he is for the present, madam, at least for the next half-hour. And concerning Mrs. Dilber and Old Joe, I should much like to add *your* name, too, to my list of comic characters, as by some mischance your name is not included in my account."

Scrooge, having drained the canister, brought it down with a crash on his little bedside-table, with such force, in fact, that his handbell almost rang all by itself.

"However," Dickens went on, ignoring the sudden clatter as he did almost all interruptions, unless they were made by his publishers, "and with your kind permission, the name of Mrs. Henrietta Gubbins may well go marching down the ages and into that dim posterity that, alas, we shall never know."

"You're not printin' my name," screeched Mrs. Gubbins, causing even Dickens to pay her some attention, "in no bleedin' book!"

"Oh, oh!" complained Scrooge, holding his head on the pillow.

Dickens came up to the other side of the bed and duelled with Mrs. Gubbins across it. "I simply do not understand it! No one wants to be identified! Not you, not Bob Cratchit . . ."

"O' course 'e don't! Creep just told me Cratchit's gonna get a knight'ood!"

"So *that's* why he wants no scandal! I think I can say he will receive no such thing! His treatment of Mr. Scrooge renders such an award impossible! Nay, unfair!"

Upon hearing that he was again the subject of discussion, Scrooge took a sip from the gin-glass that Tessie had brought and resignedly, but noisily, commenced gargling with it.

"I'm takin' this ol' gentleman 'ome!" cried Mrs. Gubbins, jerking her thumb at the burbling porpoise in the bed. "An' if, in due time, 'e should turn 'is thoughts to marriage—"

Scrooge spluttered, blew out his breath, and shot a spray of gin almost to the doorway.

"I *thought* that would surprise you," Mrs. Gubbins told Scrooge sweetly. "You'll be my *fifth*, my dear."

"God rest ye merry, gentlemen," sang the full chorus of the Paradise Hall choir from somewhere down below.

"Shuddup!" Axworthy's voice was heard to roar from somewhere downstairs, effectively silencing the defiant singers.

"O Death!" said Scrooge, trying to smother himself with his own pillow. "Sweet Death! A merciful relief!"

"I shall repair at once," announced Dickens, ignoring all interruptions and marching to the doorway, "to the offices of the *Evening Chronicle* and obtain the services of their star reporter." He turned before leaving purely, it must be said, for dramatic effect, for Dickens was a consummate actor. The young author's parting remark caused a muffled groan and a drawn-out sigh to come from the direction of the bed, for what Dickens added was, "And I promise you this, Mr. Scrooge: I shall return!"

Dickens smiled and nodded briefly as Tiny Tim and Belinda, accompanied by Zachary Makepeace, came up to the doorway. He then hurried off to Fleet Street, hub of the newspaper industry and known to Londoners as the "street of ink."

"Here's two more!" called out Makepeace, without much enthusiasm. "This place is getting as busy as Piccadilly on market day." The turnkey went back down the corridor to make absolutely certain that Dickens had left.

"Merry Christmas, Uncle Scrooge!" called Tiny Tim eagerly, as he and Belinda came in with their packages.

Scrooge lowered his pillow and brightened considerably as the children trooped over and sat on one side of his bed.

"Hello, Mrs. Gubbins," smiled Belinda.

" 'Ullo, love."

"The butler told us where they'd taken you," said Tiny Tim, taking Scrooge's hand. "Belinda and I just had to steal away! Father has no idea!"

"We took the last hansom!" said his sister. "From the stand!"

"From Father!" laughed her brother. "He didn't see!"

CALAMITOUS HAPPENINGS

*

At the moment that Tiny Tim, Belinda, Scrooge, and Mrs. Gubbins were laughing merrily at the thought of Cratchit's discomfiture, the future knight was barrelling along High Holborn in the direction of Little King William's Alley, furious that there was not a hansom to be had.

Worried that Dickens might carry out his threat and give him some unwelcome publicity in the evening paper and remembering Lord Pouncey's warning to avoid scandal at any cost, Cratchit thrust out his jaw and shouldered passers-by laden with Christmas parcels out of his way.

He turned south at Fetter Lane, walked into a porter humping vegetables, and shouted back enough abuse to make a tomato-vendor blush. Then he kicked a fallen parsnip on the pavement, sent it skidding, and pressed on relentlessly to Paradise Hall.

"And we brought you," said Tiny Tim, still laughing heartily, "some Christmas gifts!"

"Christmas presents? For me? Well, thank you, children." Excited, Scrooge took the larger of the two packages.

"Do open them while we're here!" urged Tiny Tim.

"This is really most kind of you." Scrooge tore away the wrapper. "Well, look at this! A new woollen night-hat! Just what I need!"

"I made it myself," Belinda said proudly. "Try it on!"

Scrooge happily obliged, pulling the hat in place. "Most comfortable. And now for the second package. Oh, dear, it's terribly small."

"This is from me!" exclaimed Tiny Tim, squirming with pleasure.

"Well, bless me!" said Scrooge, producing a small box. "It's a snuff-box!" He opened the box and sniffed the contents. "And filled with the very best snuff! Thank you, Tiny Tim! And you, too, Belinda!" Scrooge gave out with a few violent sneezes. "Beautiful snuff! I do believe it's clearing my head!"

But Tiny Tim and Belinda weren't finished yet.

"And we have another surprise for you! Are you ready, Belinda?" Tiny Tim raised his hand and used his forefinger as a baton. "One, two."

The Cratchit children sang lustily, "We wish you a merry Christmas, we wish you a merry—"

"Shut up!" shouted Axworthy from somewhere in the lower regions. "Keep quiet!"

"Oh, dear," grumbled Scrooge, "I do believe my headache's coming back." He sneezed again and groaned as the others watched him anxiously.

Hercules pounded into Pudding Lane, sending people diving. Those who had time managed a yell or two as the horse with a feedbag on his face charged on. Creep, grappling with the reins, was not worried that he had lost control. No, what caused him a nagging anxiety was the fact that one of the carriage's wheels was wobbling in a way as to suggest it might come off.

If you had been standing in Pudding Lane that Christmas Eve afternoon—though when Hercules clattered through it, very few people were, unless they stood well clear—when the teetering wheel actually did end its association with the Cratchit carriage and spin straight through the window of a pawn shop, if you had been present, you would doubtless have noticed the figure of an elderly man in butler's attire leave the driver's seat and sail up in the air, having abandoned ship, skyward fashion.

When Creep elected to come down, he wisely landed

in a pile of dust and other refuse that had been neatly collected by the Pudding Lane crossing-sweeper, who stood off to one side. The last thing Creep saw before he fainted was the Cratchit horse and carriage, both leaning sideways, speeding around the corner and heading down to the River Thames.

"Here's another one," Zachary Makepeace said in disgust as he ushered Dr. Erasmus Youngblood into the extremely popular Grey Room. He muttered as he trudged away, "We'll soon have more visitors here than inmates."

"Mr. Scrooge, as soon as I heard you were here, I . . ." Youngblood now noticed the love of his life. "Dear Miss Cratchit!" He swept off his hat, swept up a stool, and swept himself down onto it, close to Belinda. "How delightful it is to see you again!" the good doctor went on, scarcely able to believe his good fortune. "And so soon, so soon!"

"It is a pleasure, Doctor," said Belinda, not failing to note that her heart was throbbing madly. "A pleasure indeed! And this lady is Mrs. Gubbins."

"Oh, we met this mornin', didn't we, Doctor?" said Mrs. Gubbins, who always enjoyed chatting with the medical profession. "An' up till then, I 'ad the most astonishin' aches an' pains, but this afternoon a new one came, caught me right in the left elbow."

"I'm terribly sorry, madam, I'm afraid I only specialize in gout. That is, I hope to specialize."

"But I've 'ad gout, Doctor! I do believe I've 'ad it!"

Scrooge, who had politely cleared his throat a couple of times in a bid to attract attention, now began to cough quietly. Youngblood smiled.

"Now that would be unlikely, madam, unless you are a

blue-blood. You see, unless you are of noble birth, the incidence of gout in women is extremely rare, the male-female ratio being as high as twenty to one."

Scrooge tried a little snuff. Only Tiny Tim noticed this and held the old man's hand as Scrooge's nose braced itself, quivered in anticipation, then, goaded, erupted with a snort.

"Brilliant!" Belinda clasped her hands rapturously. "Oh, quite brilliant! What *is* gout, Doctor?"

"Gout, my dear Miss Cratchit, is one of the oldest diseases described in medical literature, just as colchicine is one of the oldest drugs in modern therapeutics. Now colchicine, of course, comes to us from colchicum, the meadow-saffron, and it is used extensively in treating the disease."

"Oh, I know *that*, Doctor," said Mrs. Gubbins airily.

"Well, why didn't you say so, just now, when this young lady asked me?"

"I didn't know *then*," admitted Mrs. Gubbins, who went on to inform Youngblood that the finest cure for gout was stout, lots of it, approximately a dozen glasses a day.

Scrooge half-closed his eyes and looked at his visitors, with the exception of Tiny Tim, a trifle balefully.

Dickens turned into the hurly-burly of Fleet Street, his favourite stamping-ground, and sniffed its delectable scents of news and gossip. In the bustling front office of the *Evening Chronicle*, where he had worked several years before, he spoke at once to a busy editor who rose eagerly and showed him the only reporter who had no assignment that afternoon, a scruffy young individual with unkempt hair, a straggling moustache, filthy fingernails, and a baggy suit of clothes, doodling in the corner and smoking a meerschaum pipe. Dickens took to him instantly, especially on hearing that the young reporter had only just joined the paper, having come all the way down from Glasgow, in Scotland. The reporter's name, Dickens learned, was Hamish Wrottenbury.

Wrottenbury listened intently to what Dickens had to say, and while he himself said nothing, Dickens noted that from time to time Wrottenbury's pipe sent up little smoke-signals of interest as he poured out the saga of Cratchit's misdeeds.

"Luncheon," cried Tessie Witherspoon, "is served." She came in through the doorway carrying a steaming dish, on the edge of which rested a spoon and a fork.

"Oh, lovely," said Scrooge, glad of the chance to interrupt his visitors. "What is it?" He burned his hands slightly as he took the dish, then held it with part of the bed-sheet.

"It's that new Eye-talian dish from the Continent," Tessie explained. "Very tasty, very 'peekwant'."

Scrooge frowned. "But it looks horrible! It looks like worms!"

"It *is* worms, love, *spaghetti*-worms, all you gotta do is suck 'em down."

"And what's that awful red stuff? What a mess!"

"You just enjoy it!" Tessie ordered, making for the doorway. "I want to see a clean plate!"

"I refuse!" called out Scrooge as Tessie disappeared. "I can't eat this! It isn't English!" He tried unsuccessfully to put a morsel on his fork. "Look at it, it keeps sliding off! It simply won't be eaten!"

"Please allow me, sir," said Tiny Tim, taking the spoon and fork and expertly twirling the delicacy. "I tasted this when you sent me to the hospital in Switzerland."

While he waited, Scrooge tried to eat a long thread of the foodstuff with his fingers, but succeeded only in plastering his chin with tomato-paste. He wiped it off with the bed-sheet only to hear the doctor's continued discourse:

"Now gout itself is a hereditary metabolic disorder characterized by recurrent acute attacks of inflammation in one or more of the extremities."

"Oh, the extremities!" said Belinda admiringly.

"Yes," Youngblood went on, noticing how demurely Belinda was gazing at him, "and gout results from the deposition, in and about the joints, of salts of uric acid, which is present in marked excess throughout the body."

"Throughout the body!" Belinda repeated dreamily.

Tiny Tim had almost completed spinning a portion of spaghetti, and Scrooge leaned back on his pillow and opened his mouth expectantly.

"And continued deposition of uric acid salts may well cause knobby deformities, and as a matter of fact, Miss Catchit—" Youngblood lightly touched Belinda's ear, and she at once became breathless and blissful "—they may also occur in the ear, right there. There, dear Miss Belinda, do you feel that?"

"Oh, yes!"

"Then I *still* say I've 'ad it!" shouted Mrs. Gubbins triumphantly. "In me foot and in me ear-'ole!" She leaned across the bed and, to Scrooge's consternation, snatched the portion twirled by Tiny Tim and devoured it.

Scrooge couldn't help but pull a face in his frustration.

Creep, staggering along on foot, was getting closer to his destination.

He was utterly dishevelled after his fall and looked a wreck, with his coat covered with dust, his shirt torn and hanging out in places, and his hair awry, all of which tended to make him look more like a dustman than a discreet and dependable butler. He took a small paper-bag from his pocket, looked inside it, and was relieved to discover that the contents were still intact.

Creep carried on, unaware that Bob Cratchit was a street ahead of him and grimly marching forward, or that Dickens and Hamish Wrottenbury, newshound extraordinaire, were bringing up the rear, all of them heading for Paradise Hall.

"Everyone's been so kind," ventured Scrooge, "but would it be possible, do you think, if I were to endeavour to get a small word in edgewise?"

At precisely the wrong moment Tiny Tim popped a spoonful of hot tomato-paste into Scrooge's mouth.

"Of course, Mr. Scrooge," said Youngblood, "but first a question. What news of my potion? Did it work?"

"Mmm . . . mmm . . . miraculous remedy . . . mmm . . . Tiny Tim, would you be kind enough to look in my belongings on the table there and see if it was included with my things?"

"Oh, yes, sir!" Tiny Tim handed Scrooge the spaghetti-dish, ran to the table, and began rummaging.

Scrooge decided to try again. "And as I was about to observe, Doctor—"

"I observe only too well that these surroundings are hardly congenial for a man in your condition. This morning, when you had a home, you were kind enough to invite me to join you there for supper. May I now invite you, sir, to enjoy a merry Christmas in a bed in Doctor Lovejoy's clinic?"

" 'E's comin' 'ome with me!" insisted Mrs. Gubbins loudly.

"Oh, I can't stand it!" Scrooge put his lunch on the bedside-table. "Merciful relief!"

"This way to the torture-chamber," Makepeace announced as he brought Bob Cratchit up to the doorway. "Straight through where all the noise is." The turnkey turned and, keys jingling like bells on a sleigh, slid off down the corridor.

"Belinda? And Timothy?!" Cratchit crossed angrily to the table, grabbed Tiny Tim, and shook him roughly. "You have defied my orders, sir, to stay in your room! I shall deal with you later!"

Cratchit marched to the bed and sat in the place Tiny Tim had vacated. Tiny Tim, wincing from the jolting, resumed searching through Scrooge's things.

"Oh, Father," said Belinda nervously. "This is Doctor Youngblood."

Cratchit was menacingly polite. "The honour is mine, Doctor." He then shouted, "And kindly remove your chair to a more appropriate distance between yourself and my daughter!"

Youngblood scowled and pulled his stool back a bit. Cratchit turned to Scrooge, who was dabbing his lips with the bed-sheet and wondering if at last he might get a word in.

"Now then. Where is that swine, Dickens? Has he been here yet?" Cratchit's frown deepened as a horrible thought occurred to him. "I can only pray he didn't go to the newspaper office first."

"No," said Mrs. Gubbins, " 'e came 'ere first, love. *Then* 'e went to the paper shop."

"What?!" Cratchit almost exploded in indignation. "How dare you? Don't you 'love' me!"

"Not at the moment," countered Mrs. Gubbins coyly, "but I could, I s'pose, if I got ta know ya."

"Sorry, Uncle Scrooge," said Tiny Tim, returning from the table and sitting at the foot of the bed, well away from his father. "No medicine there."

"Oh, dear, oh, dear," Scrooge managed to get out. He was about to ask his well-wishers if they would mind not pressing on his painful feet under the counterpane when Cratchit actually increased the pressure, leaning forward while talking in the most conciliatory fashion.

"Now look here, old chap. I know that in electing to come here, you acted in my best interests. And I must confess I had no idea that behind the façade of these premises were such sordid and drab surroundings, which I find totally unsuitable for a dear friend such as you. Therefore," Cratchit went on expansively and a shade pompously, "and after due consideration, it is my intention to move you from here and put you into much more comfortable quarters until you come home to us and are placed in the attic. The rooms I have decided to reserve for you are in a quiet and charming spot, The Peal of Bells Inn, in the Covent Garden market."

"I wouldn't stay *there!*" screeched Mrs. Gubbins, thumping Scrooge's left knee for emphasis. "You 'ear the market-porters chuckin' about their fruit an' vegetable crates all night! Stayed there on me 'oneymoon with me second! We didn't sleep a wink!"

"Please be quiet, madam!" Cratchit shouted back. "We have no desire to know about your honeymoon. Remember, there are children present." He turned back to Scrooge and lowered his voice. "I would have come here sooner, but that hideous butler of mine, Creep, had the audacity to steal my horse and carriage and go off on some mysterious and nefarious mission of his own. And now, old friend, I must hie me to the *Chronicle* and suppress the vile story that Dickens even now is undoubtedly concocting." Cratchit grasped Scrooge's hand. "Good-bye, Mr. Scrooge, for now. I'll be back to take you away from this awful place before you know it. In the meantime, old comrade, rest easy and relax."

Several pairs of feet came tramping down the corridor. Zachary Makepeace, as usual, acted as host.

"Here's a couple more!" He made the colossal mistake of adding, "I'll *never* lay hands on him at this rate."

Noel Axworthy, the Master, had come up to the doorway together with Dickens and Hamish Wrottenbury. Axworthy angrily shoved his fist in the turnkey's face. "You stop threatenin' Mr. Scrooge or I'll chivvy yer throat aht!"

Makepeace, who knew when to cringe, did so and crept away.

" 'Ere you are, Mr. Scrooge." Axworthy tossed a small box to Scrooge, who to his own surprise neatly caught it. "I brought you some more 'eadache powders. You might like to keep the box 'andy." The Master stood behind the bed and folded his arms grimly. "An' this time I intends to stay, to see me interests is protected."

On seeing Dickens, Cratchit jumped up, incensed. "Dickens! How dare you return to these private accommodations?" Cratchit stared, aghast, at Dickens's scruffy, pipe-smoking companion. "And who is this filthy tramp you've brought with you?"

The young reporter answered for himself and spoke in the hideous accent exclusive to those who are born and raised in the equally hideous district of Glasgow known as Gorbals. "Ah canna waste ma time i' tradin' insults." Wrottenbury sat on the other side of the bed, close to Scrooge, and puffed a cloud of foul-smelling fumes in Scrooge's face. "Not if ma reporrrt is tae mak' the last edition."

"Did he just say 'last edition'?" Cratchit echoed. "So! A *scribe*! I tell you I'll not stand for it!"

And Cratchit sat. Dickens sat behind Wrottenbury. Scrooge began to feel quite hemmed in. He opened his box of powders, untied a twist, and asked Mrs. Gubbins for a little more gin. She handed him the glass, and Scrooge gulped from it gratefully as more pipe-smoke billowed over him. "Merciful relief! And it started out as such a quiet day!"

"Now then," said Wrottenbury, pulling out a notebook and pencil from what he considered his best suit of clothes (though it was, in fact, one of the shabbiest in London). "Which one o' these gentlemen is Mr. Scrudge?"

"The only one wearin' a night-cap, dear," said Mrs. Gubbins, who was probably the only one who had properly understood the young reporter, her fourth and final husband having been a Scot.

"This gentleman," said Dickens, "is Mr. Hamish Wrottenbury, of the *Evening Chronicle*. Formerly with the *Glasgow Echo* and the *Edinburgh Gleaner*. Please get on with it, Hamish. I'll not interrupt."

"Now then, Mr. Scrudge," began Wrottenbury, his pencil poised. "Where were ye borrrn—and when?"

"Ask me why, ask me why!" Scrooge's anguished outburst was followed by a slightly sarcastic question, which he put to Dickens. "Did you say you were bringing me the *Chronicle*'s star reporter?"

" 'E looks more to me," said Mrs. Gubbins, who understandably, in the light of her recent marital experience, did not care much for people from Scotland, "like a pox-doctor's clerk."

"An' you should know, woman!" shouted Wrottenbury. "Away an' shu' yer face!"

Scrooge spluttered as more clouds rolled over him.

"But I really have no desire to be interviewed! I don't want any harm to come to my old friend, dear Bob Cratchit."

Cratchit rewarded Scrooge by thumping his back enthusiastically and with such force as to cause him almost to vomit. "Well said, Ebenezer! Don't tell him anything! And before you know it, some time in January we'll have you boarded up, all on your own and safe from everybody, way up in the attic."

"I was born," Scrooge now decided to tell Wrottenbury, "in the village of Little Tarkington, in Oxfordshire, in the year seventeen hundred and seventy-three."

"Now we're gettin' somewhere," said Wrottenbury, writing furiously as Cratchit clutched his face in dismay. "An' who did this terrible thing to you, Mr. Scrudge?"

"Well, my parents, of course."

"Och, no!" cried Wrottenbury impatiently. "Ah mean today!"

Dickens, who had promised not to interrupt, did. "I have already acquainted Mr. Wrottenbury with the brief details, Mr. Scrooge, and all he wants now is to ask you one or two more questions."

"Don't tell him anything!" pleaded Cratchit, tugging at Scrooge's arm. "I'm begging you, beseeching you!"

"Even if he wasna tae tell me a worrrd," said Wrottenbury, writing and puffing, "his vairy presence here is sufficient fer a story. Ah know he used tae reside wi' you, an' that's guid enough fer me." The reporter now read out what he had written in his book. "Elderly gent sent tae workhouse fer Christmas . . . City businessman exposed by famous author . . . An exclusive *Chronicle* report."

Cratchit gasped like a landed whale. "But you can't print that!"

"Ye'd be amazed, Mr. Cratchit, sir," said Wrottenbury

with a quiet smile of triumph, "at wha' a filthy tramp can get up to."

As Wrottenbury resumed writing, Cratchit made a mental note to himself that the only solution available to him, and one that had been highly recommended to him when dealing with awkward and difficult members of the press, would be to resort to that good old standby, bribery.

The light was fading fast outside Paradise Hall as dusk, and Creep, approached.

Still looking like some awful apparition, Creep opened the side-door and tottered in. Behind the grille, Mrs. Axworthy looked up from her register and, on seeing the dust-covered ghost before her, gave a groan of horror, eased the considerable strain on her squinting eyes, and slid from her stool to the floor. Her last thought before blacking out was to go much easier on the gooseberry wine in the future.

The imperturbable Creep calmly reached through the gap in the grille, snatched up Mrs. Axworthy's wine-flask, and gulped down some of the refreshing liquid. He then leaned against the counter and brushed himself with his free hand in a poor attempt to dust himself off.

When the flask had been relieved of its contents, Creep tidily replaced it on the desk, picked up the bundle of keys that happened to be lying handy, and sneaked cautiously to the double-doors that led to the upper regions of Paradise Hall. Dazed though he was, he was determined to find a certain kind old gentleman and give him the potion in his pocket that he needed for his gout.

Dickens held the despatch-case containing his manuscript above the crowded bed and tapped it meaningfully.

"Of course there's one way, Mr. Cratchit, to guarantee that no unfavourable report about you appears. Grant me permission to use your actual name in my charming Christmas story; you'll be surprised at what a little co-operation will do, sir. I'm just going round to my publishers now. However," he added knowingly, "if you're not really *interested* in obtaining a knighthood—"

Cratchit had been following Dickens's words with slowly widening eyes and now reacted violently. "My knighthood! Who told you about that, sir?" He lunged at Scrooge, who shrank back on his pillow. "Was it you? Was it you?"

"You leave 'im alone!" Mrs. Gubbins pulled Cratchit's hands away, restraining him. "You'd strike yer old employer! If you wanna know, *I* told 'im! An' yer butler told *me*! The one 'oo ran away with yer 'orse an' cart!"

"Creep?!" A murderous light began to flash in Cratchit's eyes. "I shall discharge him!"

"Oh, don't do that, Father!" urged Tiny Tim.

"We like him, we love him!" seconded Belinda.

Cratchit's response was to reach down the bed and try to bang his children's heads together. Scrooge, now badly crushed under the counterpane, let out a cry. Dr. Youngblood at once eased the pressure, pulling Cratchit firmly and decisively back.

"Pray do not harm Miss Belinda," the good doctor advised Cratchit, "or I shall be obliged to intervene."

"How dare you presume to call my daughter 'Miss Belinda'? And kindly inform that old ass, Doctor Lovejoy, that he is no longer my doctor! And neither are you!"

"Oh, no, please, Father." But Cratchit ignored Belinda and began jabbing determinedly at Dickens.

"As for you, I shall not yield to your blackmail demand! You shall *not* have my permission! I prefer to be known as Algernon Muddlecombe! And Mr. Scrooge will be Gregory Flintlock!"

"Oh, would that I were!" panted Scrooge. He then added, somewhat confusedly: "Who's *he?*"

"Now let me get these names right, the noo." Wrottenbury, puzzled, referred to his notes. "Ah distinctly remember thinkin' yer name was Scrudge."

Creep reached the landing. He paused and listened to the shouts that were coming from way down the corridor, but as these were too far away to be understood, he concluded that some sort of Christmas party must be going on.

Having never been in the corridor before, Creep decided to unlock and unbolt the first door he came across, just in case Mr. Scrooge was behind it. As he pushed the door back, an old man in rags shuffled out, grinned hugely as if unable to believe his good fortune, and hurried downstairs without a word.

Creep moved on to the second door. When he opened it, a fat, middle-aged woman looked out; she beamed, grabbed Creep, dragged him into her room, and slammed the door. After a moment her door opened and the bundle of keys that Creep had been carrying hit the corridor floor. The door slammed again.

Zachary Makepeace, attracted by the unusual sound of doors being opened and closed, came down the corridor to investigate. The turnkey stooped and, scratching his head, picked up the bundle of keys as the shouting in the Grey Room continued.

"I shall not yield," Cratchit informed Dickens, repeatedly digging at the author's upper arm, "though I lose my knighthood! Even a Mister can have integrity. Mr. Scrooge himself taught me that." Cratchit came to a decision and turned to Scrooge, who, unnoticed by the others, was near to tears. "Pack up your things, old chap. You're coming home with me."

"But the attic—Tiny Tim tells me there are mice up there!" Scrooge was petrified at the very thought of sharing quarters with the scurrying little creatures.

" 'E isn't goin' anywhere!" Axworthy stepped forward, angrily unfolding his arms. " 'E's an inmate now! Not less I gets proper compensation!" Scrooge winced.

"You will be paid, man!" snapped Dickens, who then addressed Scrooge gently. "You're coming home with me to my house in Devonshire Terrace. We'll talk." Scrooge shuddered.

Mrs. Gubbins intervened. " 'E's comin' 'ome wi' *me* to Mincin' Lane!" Scrooge blanched.

"Well," ventured Youngblood, "*I* had thought about Doctor Lovejoy's clinic." Scrooge frowned.

"Oh, yes!" Belinda happily confirmed. "And I can visit him there!" Scrooge trembled.

"Isn't anyone," Scrooge asked plaintively, "going to ask me what *I* want to do?"

"Tessie will!" Grinning delightedly, the oldest surviving inmate hurried in through the doorway. "Oh, stay where you are, sir, stay where you are!"

Axworthy seized and shook her roughly. "Shove orf! 'E isn't stayin'! Not less I gets compensation!" He threw Tessie out into the corridor with quite considerable force.

"Oh, the poor creature," said Scrooge with genuine concern. "I really must see if she's well."

Scrooge rang the handbell. Makepeace appeared in the doorway holding Creep by the scruff of his neck and literally hurled the butler into the room.

Creep enquired automatically, "You rang, sir?"

"Creep!" Cratchit flew into a rage on seeing his

unkempt and dishevelled servant. "What are *you* doing here?"

"Oh, sir, Mr. Scrooge forgot his potion!" Creep pulled the paper-bag from his pocket, removed the precious jar, and gave it to Scrooge. "I didn't want to think of you possibly suffering, sir, so I thought I'd bring it post-haste."

"Merciful relief," Scrooge exclaimed, immediately helping himself to a spoonful. "God bless you, Creep!"

"Why," Cratchit persisted, "did you take my horse and carriage? I demand to know!"

"I was rather hoping you wouldn't notice they'd gone, sir."

"Wouldn't notice? Why do you look like that?"

"Well, Hercules—that is, your thoroughbred gelding, sir—elected to leave without me. And a little later a wheel came off, sir. It was only one of the rear wheels. On the left side."

"You clumsy oaf, Creep! Where's my carriage now?"

"It seemed so strange, sir, to observe it leaning over to one side and speeding around the corner that leads out of Pudding Lane, then heading straight down to Puddle Dock, which, as you are probably aware, sir, is quite close to the Blackfriars Bridge."

"WHAT?!" The word rang out like a pistol-shot; it was at this point that Scrooge, having gulped down his potion, began to shake in the bed like a man with malaria.

"I said," Creep replied politely, "it seemed so strange to observe your carriage leaning over to one side, as it were, and hurtling around the corner of Pudding Lane, and then—"

"You're discharged, Creep! Dismissed from my household staff!"

"Oh, pray don't sack me! Just give me a good talking-to, sir, it'll do me more good! It's Christmas Eve, you can't discharge me now! After all my long and faithful service!"

Cratchit's face turned from red to purple. "You've only been with me for two and a half months!"

"Oh, sir," said Creep, bursting into tears, "does this mean you won't be paying me a pension? Oh, little did I think, when I was a lad of eight, setting off fifty-seven years ago from Bristol to seek my fortune, that it would ever come to this! Sacked, aye, and sacked at Christmas!"

"Christmas?" Scrooge yelled the word, clenched his fists, and shadow-boxed in the air. "Bah! Humbug! There, I've said it!" And having said it, he fell back and hit his head on the Grey Room's iron bed-rail.

"Oh, there must be some way," Scrooge moaned pitifully, "that I can be left in peace . . . I know, I have it!" He rang the handbell like a man inspired, and Tessie, now smiling again, rushed in. "Tessie, will you be kind enough to get me a bedpan?"

As if on a command to stand to attention, Scrooge's visitors immediately rose.

"And hurry, Tessie," he went on, encouraged by this, "my need is desperate! Merciful relief!"

"And which paper would you like with it, sir?" Tessie enquired. "The *Times* or the *Gazette*?"

"The *Chronicle*!" Scrooge threw a dark look at Wrottenbury. "The *Evening Chronicle*! 'Twill be a pleasure!"

Tessie hurried out, as did everyone else except Dickens.

"When may we know your intention, sir?" Dickens asked. "With which one of us will you elect to stay? Let me know at your convenience."

"I shall let you know," Scrooge responded, having misunderstood, "down at the front door! And now kindly leave me, leave me."

Dickens nodded and went out. Scrooge was now alone. "Oh, peace at last! It's heavenly. All on my own-e-o!"

He threw back the counterpane, swung out his legs, and sat on the edge of the bed, at the same time becoming aware that a distant clanking sound was growing louder and, therefore, getting closer to his doorway. He glanced over and saw Zachary Makepeace. The turnkey entered stealthily, his hands itching for a throat.

"So you think you're going, Scrooge, do you? Do you think I'll allow you to escape from me now?" Makepeace gave a hoarse chuckle and came menacingly up to the bed. "Never! We'll settle accounts. And I only owed you five pounds ten!"

Scrooge rose in terror as he remembered Axworthy's description of the turnkey's attack upon an inmate. "Oh, them 'ands! Them terrible 'ands!" he wailed. "No, Zachary, no!"

"I'll swing for you, you old sinner." Makepeace hurled his hands at Scrooge's neck. "These hands'll snap your throat!"

Scrooge managed a small cry before he lost the power of speech. Makepeace dragged him up the bed and down the bed as Scrooge struggled in vain. The bedside-table went over, handbell, spaghetti-dish, soup-canister, gin-glass, and all. Makepeace and Scrooge ignored the clatter and went grimly about their business, the victim trying helplessly to resist while the attacker made a thoroughly good job of wringing, throttling, and choking.

Tessie Witherspoon rushed in. She had heard the bedside-table go over and now raised the bedpan she had brought and clubbed Makepeace with it from behind. There was a resounding "Dong!" as the turnkey, dazed, fell to the floor. Scrooge lay prostrate on the bed. Tessie looked anxiously at him.

"Oh, he doesn't want a bedpan now!" she shouted. " 'E's motionless!"

Being the good servant he really was, Creep was the first of the visitors to respond to the commotion. He ran into the Grey Room and sat on the now-blinking Makepeace, doing his best to restrain him. But it was a losing fight, the turnkey being infinitely more powerful.

"Oh, I can't 'old 'im!" Creep howled at the doorway. "Mr. Cratchit! Doctor!"

Cratchit came in and held Makepeace down. Dr. Youngblood went to the bed and examined Scrooge. Behind them came Tiny Tim, Belinda, Axworthy, Dickens, and Wrottenbury with, of course, his notebook at the ready.

"Wha' a story!" exclaimed the reporter, taking in the tragic scene. "An *Evenin' Chronicle* exclusive! Is he dead?"

"Don't you worry your head about him," Makepeace leered from the floor. "He's dead and done for. Mr. Scrooge'll never see another merry Christmas."

Mrs. Gubbins appeared in the doorway. She had heard the turnkey's remark, and she hurried over to her old friend in the bed, shouting: "Say it isn't true! Mr. Scrooge! Mr. Scrooge!"

But the old man just lay there, pale and still, his eyes closed and his mouth open. Dr. Youngblood, his examination concluded, turned to the others and sadly shook his head.

Twenty minutes after her shock and fainting-fit, Gloria Axworthy staggered to her feet. She gripped the edge of the counter and stared in disbelief as the doors at the back of the reception-area suddenly parted.

A stretcher holding the blanket-covered figure of Scrooge was carried in by her husband and Dr. Youngblood. Scrooge still wore the new night-hat he'd been given for Christmas; beneath the blanket he now had on his night-shirt. Creep came in behind the stretcher-bearers with Scrooge's belongings piled high in his arms, and behind the old butler were Mrs. Gubbins and Belinda, both weeping quietly. Bob Cratchit, Tiny Tim, and Dickens solemnly brought up the rear.

Mrs. Axworthy poured herself a non-existent drink from the flask Creep had emptied, devoutly crossed herself, and gulped from the glass, refreshing herself with nothing.

The question an impartial observer might have asked, had there been one present and impartially observing, was this: what had become of that awful newsman, Hamish Wrottenbury?

The Scotsman had slipped away to the offices of the *Evening Chronicle*, determined not to miss the important last edition's deadline. He babbled his version of the murderous attack, not forgetting to add what he had heard concerning Cratchit's impending knighthood, to an eager editor, who at once put the reporter's torrent of words into more acceptable and therefore much plainer English—which is to say, journalese.

Within the hour, after the presses had rolled out their latest scandals and after raucous newsboys had joyfully sung their praises in the streets—"Another 'orrible murder! Read all about it!"—Londoners settled down to enjoy the sordid details of Scrooge's demise and Cratchit's disaster.

London, it must regretfully be said, thrives on a sensation or two every twenty-four hours, and there were many, I fear, who found Wrottenbury's twin-scoops sweet and cheering reading, coming, as they did, just in nice time for Christmas, and all for a few pennies, too.

GOD BLESS US EVERY ONE!

And for those *Evening Chronicle* readers who bore Scrooge or Cratchit a grudge, whether rightly or wrongly, then this particular Christmas would be their merriest in years.

3

The Calamity Resolved

An imposing-looking man sat behind an even more imposing-looking desk, reading his copy of the *Evening Chronicle* with growing stupefaction.

Sir Robert Peel, Prime Minister of England, suddenly hurled the newspaper to one side and reached for a document on his desk bearing the heading "New Year's Honours List" and containing several dozen names, neatly arranged in alphabetical order.

The Prime Minister's pen plunged into an inkwell, surfaced, soared, then swooped down on the document, feverishly scratching out the name "Cratchit, Robert." Then, grunting and trembling with rage, he tugged a bell-rope that hung on the wall just behind him.

What sounded like the chimes of Big Ben immediately boomed out, striking six times, and this wasn't surprising, for it was precisely six o'clock. The distinguished Prime Minister rested his elbows on the desk and viciously twisted his hands as he waited for his flunkey to answer his ring.

The lamplighters left Mountjoy Square ablaze, and they now made their flickering way to adjoining, less-important streets to brighten their darkness for Christmas.

Inside Bob Cratchit's house, where many more decorations had been added, the face of Scrooge was slowly sinking. Daisy, the maid, stood on a chair by the fireplace where, assisted by Mrs. Cratchit, who held the chair, she lowered Scrooge's portrait from its place over the mantel. Both Daisy and her mistress were glum.

"Poor Mr. Scrooge!" said Daisy tearfully. "Oh, it seems such a shame, madam."

"Then this really is the end of him," said Mrs. Cratchit, reaching for a chocolate with her free hand. "Christmas won't seem Christmas without dear old Mr. Scrooge."

Mrs. Cratchit took the portrait from Daisy, leaned it against the chair, and handed up to the maid the portrait's replacement, a framed painting of Queen Victoria.

"Well, them was Mr. Cratchit's orders to me, madam, 'fore 'e went out," explained Daisy, putting the Queen in place. " 'Take down Scrooge,' says 'e to me, 'an' 'ang 'Er Majesty in time for the party tonight.' "

"The Queen," said Mrs. Cratchit loyally, swallowing a gin-soaked fig. "God bless her."

"An' where's Mr. Creep, I'd like to know?" complained Daisy, balancing herself on the chair. " 'E should be doin' this."

"And where's Mr. Cratchit," asked Mrs. Cratchit, quickly supporting Daisy, "and my darling children? Missing for hours!"

"Is she quite straight, madam?" Daisy meant the Queen.

Mrs. Cratchit carefully checked. "So I do believe."

Daisy skipped down and picked up the portrait that had fallen from Bob Cratchit's favour. "And where shall I put Mr. Scrooge, madam?"

"Now let me see ..." Mrs. Cratchit had what she believed to be a flash of inspiration. "Put him in the attic."

"Very good, madam." Daisy put the chair back in its place and was moving with Scrooge's portrait to the staircase when someone beat on the front door with what was, in fact, a silver-topped stick.

Daisy admitted Lord Pouncey, chairman of the York-shire Penny Bank, who marched in angrily with a news-paper under his arm. Daisy put Scrooge down and took his lordship's things.

"Oh, good evening, Lord Pouncey," smiled Mrs. Cratchit, coming over. "You are indeed early for the party, but you are welcome, sir, nonetheless."

"It is with regret that I must tell you I shall not attend your party!" Pouncey flourished the newspaper. "I have come to confront your husband! With this!"

Daisy took Scrooge to join the mice up in the attic.

"I'm afraid you will have to confront *me* with it, whatever it is." Mrs. Cratchit politely led Pouncey to the fire. "My husband is out."

"Ha! I am not surprised. I have come straight from the residence of the Prime Minister himself. Oh, he was terribly upset."

"Upset? But why, my lord?"

"Your husband's knighthood is now in the gravest jeopardy!" Pouncey bristled. "In fact, it's in serious doubt."

"You mean I shan't be a lady after all?"

"I mean precisely that!" Lord Pouncey held up the final edition of the *Evening Chronicle* and struck the front page several times with the back of his hand. "The evening paper, madam! It has headlines to make the blood dance!"

Mrs. Cratchit gripped the back of a chair and sounded quite faint. "The evening paper?"

"Not since Trafalgar have I seen such lurid and shocking headlines! Your husband is guilty of the most astonishing breach of etiquette, a breach that has compromised the Prime Minister, to say nothing of Her Most Gracious Majesty! Listen to this, ma'am, and if I were you, I'd have my smelling-salts handy!"

"Daisy!" Mrs. Cratchit sounded like a Swiss yodelling in fear of an avalanche. "Daisy! My salts!"

Daisy hurried downstairs to the sideboard, brought out a small bottle, opened it, and held it under Mrs. Cratchit's nose, at the same time generally supporting her mistress.

"The first headline is ..." Pouncey paused for effect, then for even greater effect added, "Are you sure you wouldn't prefer to sit, ma'am?"

Mrs. Cratchit bravely shook her head, but held on tightly to the back of the chair.

"Very well. Now listen to *this* for the most sensational news in years." Pouncey cleared his throat and read, very sombrely: " 'Mild Disturbance at City Workhouse.' "

"Oh!" cried Mrs. Cratchit, gasping with surprise. "Oh, oh! You are indeed right, Lord Pouncey, it is shocking indeed!" She might have fainted, had not the efficient Daisy been ready with the salts, giving her mistress several generous whiffs and sniffs.

"There's more. And the second headline is much, much worse." Pouncey read out, with a good deal of relish: " 'Altercation at Paradise Hall.' "

"That's where Mr. Scrooge was taken! No more, please, I beg of you!"

"I must. The third headline: 'Elderly Inmate Throttled by Turnkey.' "

"They must mean Mr. Scrooge!" Mrs. Cratchit fell backwards; Daisy was ready with a chair. "Oh, the poor man! And we've only just put his portrait in the attic!"

"And the final headline is the most telling of all. I almost said 'damning', but out of deference to your presence I decided not to say it. The final headline: 'New Year's Honours List to be Revised.' " Lord Pouncey lowered the newspaper and added, as though all his senses had been shattered, "I can't go on."

"Oh, my poor husband!" Mrs. Cratchit wailed. "The disgrace, the ignominy!"

At the same time that Mrs. Cratchit was bemoaning her husband's fate, Creep, having of course come in by the tradesmen's entrance, was down in the kitchen being slowly turned around and vigorously brushed by Mrs. Summerhayes, the cook, at the same time sipping, as dust flew around him, a much-needed schooner of his master's vintage port. His shirt and cravat were back in place, and what little hair he had was tidy again.

"And I've nowhere to go except here, Mrs. Summerhayes," said Creep, wishing the good lady wouldn't keep pulling down his drinking-arm, "nowhere, nowhere, nowhere. Could you pack me enough sandwiches to last me over Christmas? And some wine, just a few bottles. And a pudding or two. And some rope. And a little poison, nice poison. Oh, and put in a carving knife, will you? I'm losing my home. There's no place like home when there's nowhere else to go."

The cook ignored all this and kept brushing. When she had flicked the last fleck, Creep sank the schooner

decisively and made for his listening-post on the servants'
stairs.

"Naturally," Creep heard Lord Pouncey remark to Mrs.
Cratchit, "the Prime Minister sent for me at once. It was I,
I am afraid, who had put your husband's name forward in
the first place. It was I who mistakenly recommended he
should receive such an honour."

Mrs. Cratchit was stung by this statement, and she
retorted with considerable sarcasm. "Yes, I well remember
my husband investing in your new brick-works, my lord."

"If I had but known! This, I fear, will reflect upon me."

"I'm absolutely sure it will, my lord."

"I warned you to avoid any scandal! And the Prime
Minister demands to know why news of the knighthood
was revealed so early! Revealed to the press in advance!"

Creep did not care at all for the manner in which his
mistress was being addressed, so he decided to go up and
enter the living-room. He padded in, pottering and
sniffing discreetly.

"Creep!" Mrs. Cratchit called out at once. She rose and
came over to him. "Thank goodness you're back. Have you
seen my husband?"

"Yes, madam," Creep replied brokenly. "I've been
discharged." He placed one foot on the main stairway's
first step. "I only came back to get my things and say
good-bye."

Mrs. Cratchit was most surprised. "*Good-bye*, Creep?"

"Good-bye, madam." Creep sadly started upstairs.

"Back down here and explain!" Mrs. Cratchit commanded him. "I don't understand you, Creep. I never
have."

Creep came back down. "Oh, madam, I was discharged

at Paradise Hall! For wrecking Mr. Cratchit's beautiful carriage."

"That old thing?" Mrs. Cratchit waved her hand impatiently. "Who cares about that? What on earth happened to Mr. Scrooge?"

"The poor old gentleman was choked, madam." Creep was near to tears. "I'm afraid he's very close to breathing his last."

"Good lord!" exclaimed Lord Pouncey, horrified. "D'you mean the old devil is still alive?"

Mrs. Cratchit froze. She was now, she had decided—and her mind was quite made up—finished forever with this pompous and callous representative of the so-called upper class. In fact, such a wave of indignation swept over her, she barely heard what Creep was saying to his lordship.

"I mean, my lord," Creep responded with dignity, for he, too, had been offended by the outburst, "that Mr. Scrooge was taken for urgent medical attention to Doctor Lovejoy's clinic. On a stretcher. It took two men to carry it, my lord. One at each end."

"Scrooge alive, you say! This really ruins everything. That scandal-sheet of a newspaper has the story wrong." Lord Pouncey then made the mistake of saying to Mrs. Cratchit, "If Scrooge lives, your husband is dead, ma'am. There will be no point whatever in my pleading with the Prime Minister now. I shall have no reason to!"

To Lord Pouncey's surprise, Mrs. Cratchit responded by clapping her hands together smartly as if she'd come to a decision. Then she walked abruptly away from him towards the front door. "Daisy! Get my things! And yours, too, you're coming with me."

Daisy entered the cloakroom and brought out bonnets

and capes, which she and her determined mistress both swiftly donned. Mrs. Cratchit addressed Creep earnestly and quietly. "Was Mr. Scrooge able to speak?"

"Yes, all he said was 'Oh!' Those were his exact words, madam."

"I mean, did he request anything?"

"He did," Creep confirmed, "but we thought he was delirious! Every time they told him they'd have him right by Christmas, every time they even mentioned Christmas, he kept calling out one word."

"What was it?"

"Kept calling out for one of those funny little buttery peppermints, madam, you know the ones! It seems he has an overpowering craving for them. So I bought him a bag. Placed it on his chest."

Lord Pouncey, irritated by Mrs. Cratchit's sudden about-face and because he was being ignored, felt it was time to make his presence decidedly felt and in no unlordly fashion.

"May I ask where you are going, madam?" he boomed, fully intending to sound impolite and command her respectful attention. "Remember, I am a guest here."

"To see," replied Mrs. Cratchit, tying her bonnet grimly and nodding her approval as Daisy opened the front door. "And I pray I may be in time—a wonderful and fine old gentleman! And the next time you meet Sir Robert Peel, will you kindly tell him he may keep his knighthood, for we now discover we have no desire to have it!"

Lord Pouncey puffed and spluttered with anger. And his resentment boiled when Mrs. Cratchit went on, "And Creep, if this gentleman should choose to remain here for a time, you may offer him a glass of sherry, and when he has partaken of his sherry, you may show this gentleman out!"

"But I've been sacked, madam! The master said so!"

Mrs. Cratchit pulled down her bonnet's brim resolutely and sailed out with Daisy into Mountjoy Square. "You may leave the master to me! Come, Daisy! To Doctor Lovejoy's clinic!"

Creep closed the door behind them, trembling in the hope that he might be reinstated. Lord Pouncey marched over to the fireplace, his face red with rage.

Daisy and Mrs. Cratchit found that it was snowing, and both began to wish that they had brought along their muffs. Over on the far side of the square a torch-lit group of carollers were moving from house to house, singing blissfully and fervently and collecting for the poor. Many were laughing, too, from the sheer joy that Christmas was nearly here and that it was snowing.

As Mrs. Cratchit and Daisy turned the corner, an ornate and splendid silver-grey carriage, drawn by two snooty, head-tossing black horses, came gliding through the snowflakes, and a sharp command rang out.

"Stop here, Hoskins!"

The driver obeyed, and the horses—for they were beautifully trained as well as elegantly groomed—stopped willingly and with alacrity and didn't even pant.

Charles Dickens climbed out. Smiling and confident, he had good reason to be cheerful, for he was immensely pleased with himself. This, he couldn't help but feel, would be a Christmas to remember. Once on the pavement he turned, his cape billowing, spoke quietly and reassuringly to someone sitting in his carriage, and courteously re-moved his hat.

The distant carollers swung into "Joy to the World," and their choice of song seemed to blend perfectly with Dickens's boyish good spirits and actually heighten his enjoyment of this most delicious moment.

Dickens had turned to speak with Tessie Witherspoon, the oldest surviving inmate of Paradise Hall, of whom Noel Axworthy, the Master, had said, "She's never yet set foot out o' Paradise 'All . . . Never will." He didn't know his Dickens!

Tessie, wearing a hat and cloak that Dickens had bought from Mrs. Axworthy, gripped the top of the carriage window as she sat and listened to what her hero had to say. Although Tessie had a smile on her face that could be said to be almost as wide as Broad Street, it must be added that there were also tears, which she happily wiped away with an already well-soaked handkerchief. She was free.

"Would you care, sir," Creep asked Lord Pouncey drily, "to have a sherry before you go?"

"You call me 'my lord', not 'sir'! And yes, damn it, I do care for a sherry! And hurry up!"

As Creep busied himself at the sideboard, Pouncey glanced up at Queen Victoria's portrait over the mantel. He remarked, almost to himself, "Well, at least they've had the decency to take the old villain down and replace him with someone eminently respectable."

"Perhaps," ventured Creep, clinking the decanter, "that can always be rectified later, my lord."

"What? How dare you? Don't you dare to be insolent with me."

"Quite so, my lord." Creep came over with his tray.

"The Queen!" Lord Pouncey snatched up the sherry-glass and toasted the portrait as someone banged the front door's knocker. "God bless her."

"And her dear Prince Albert," muttered Creep, heading for the door. "And his dotty relations. And his cotton socks."

The butler smiled on seeing that the caller was Dickens and took the author's hat.

"Ah, Creep, good evening. I must commend you on your bravery this afternoon."

"His bravery, sir?" Lord Pouncey, curious, came half-way across the living-room. "The fellow's a half-wit. Who are you?"

Creep swallowed his pride, as butlers must on occasion, knowing it was his duty to introduce the two men. But he did it grudgingly as he shook the snow from Dickens's hat, simply saying, "Lord Pouncey—Mr. Charles Dickens."

"Not the author-fellow?" His lordship was displeased.

"Not the Pouncey who makes impassioned speeches in the House of Lords calling every right-thinking person's attention to the plight of the poor?" Pouncey, not without pride, nodded assent, though he quickly scowled when Dickens added, "Speeches that everyone promptly forgets?"

"Now look here! I introduced a bill, sir, increasing the minimum age at which children are allowed to work in the coal-mines from six years to seven!"

"And it was defeated," Dickens responded pleasantly, "by your own party."

"It was felt it would have added to the burden of the poor! Less wages for working families! I confess I am becoming a trifle weary, Dickens, of your endless propaganda."

"All writing is propaganda, my lord. Even yours."

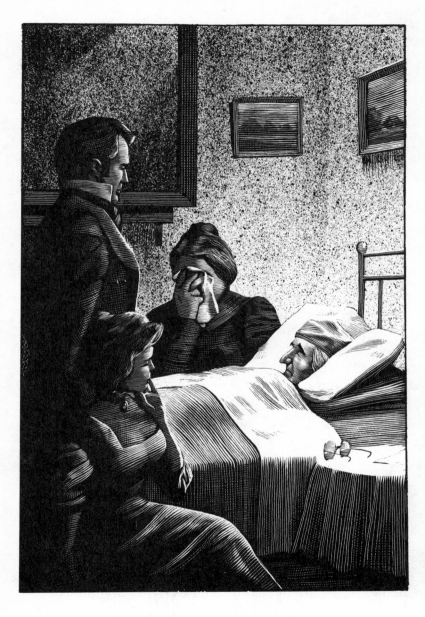

Scrooge closed his eyes again. He would say no more. Mrs. Cratchit looked up forlornly and stopped wiping his forehead.

THE CALAMITY RESOLVED

Dickens accepted a glass of sherry from Creep. "Ah, thank you." He turned back to Pouncey. "This gentleman helped to subdue a madman this afternoon."

"You have the effrontery to call a butler a *gentleman?* In front of me?"

"Why not, my lord?" Dickens placed his hand on Creep's shoulder and addressed the butler gently. "And I have good news concerning that gallant lady, Miss Tessie Witherspoon, who managed to fell the blackguard who attacked Mr. Scrooge. I have secured her release from Paradise Hall and have engaged her as my scullery-maid at my house in Devonshire Terrace. She's waiting outside in my carriage now, and wide-eyed with wonderment. The poor creature has never yet looked out in freedom on London nor even wandered at liberty abroad in it."

Creep's grin grew almost as wide as Tessie's; the old servant was extremely pleased. "That is indeed a wonderful thing to do, sir!"

Dickens gave a positively dazzling, if immodest, smile. "Yes, it *is*, isn't it? I like to think so, too."

Dickens laughed. Creep laughed. Lord Pouncey reflected that they must *both* be half-wits.

Scrooge was the only patient in Dr. Lovejoy's tiny clinic that evening, but no fewer than five anxious people watched over his bed, straining to see signs of the slightest interest in life. The friends who cared so deeply for him were Mrs. Cratchit, who had just arrived there with Daisy; Dr. Youngblood and Belinda, whose romance was for the moment forgotten; and, of course, Tiny Tim, biting his lip in the fear that Death might be abroad on this wintry night and might feel constrained to call.

If love alone could have revived the old man, then the outpouring of this intangible commodity around his narrow bed would surely have been sufficient to galvanize ten dying men and send them gambolling round their beds while revelling in a roundelay. And this love Scrooge sensed, for now, as Mrs. Cratchit touched his brow with a towel and softly drew it along the furrows, his eyes fluttered open, and he reached to grasp her hand.

A sign of life! All leaned forward as Mrs. Cratchit listened to what Scrooge was trying to whisper. Whatever he said was something the others didn't catch; but Mrs. Cratchit had heard, for her ear was close to his lips, and she nodded sadly and whispered something back.

Scrooge closed his eyes again. He would say no more. Mrs. Cratchit looked up forlornly and stopped wiping his forehead.

Bob Cratchit stamped up the snowy steps to his own front door and went in without wiping his feet. He did not immediately notice the two visitors in the living-room and, believing he had discharged his butler from his service, threw his own things onto the hat-stand.

Creep came nervously up behind him. "Beg pardon, sir ..."

"Creep! What are you doing still here?"

"Oh, sir, the mistress reinstated me." Creep hopefully tidied Cratchit's things on the stand.

"We'll see about that. Where is she now?"

"Oh, sir," Creep nodded towards the living-room, indicating that there were visitors present, then went to his post on the servants' stairs.

"Pouncey?" exclaimed Cratchit, grimly approaching him. "And *Dickens*?!"

"You have seen," thundered Lord Pouncey, "the evening paper, sir?"

"I have. I've just come from the *Evening Chronicle*

office now. I wanted the chief editor to publish a retraction. I failed."

"Failed, sir? Why did you fail?"

"A horrible card was in the window saying 'Closed for Christmas—next news on Boxing Day'! I marched up and down Fleet Street searching for the editor in all the wine shops and ale-houses! And then I found *him*, that awful Scotsman, Hamish Wrottenbury, stinking out The Cheshire Cheese with his foul-smelling meerschaum and drunk on Irish whiskey! I ask you, what sort of Scotsman is that, drinking the brew from the bogs? So I brandished his own filthy rag under his nose, and when I informed him that he had the story wrong, that Scrooge still lived, he nearly swallowed his pipe! He then dashed off to Marylebone Station to make enquiries concerning the next available train to Glasgow, saying he had an urgent desire to return to the Scottish hag who calls herself his mother!"

"The Prime Minister is much distressed," Lord Pouncey said bleakly. "There'll be no knighthood now."

"What further news," Dickens asked pleasantly, coming between the two men, "concerning Mr. Scrooge?"

Not even the young author's vivid imagination could have foreseen such a startling reaction, for Cratchit now flew into a flaring temper and towering rage. "What news of Mr. Scrooge? Is that all you find to care about?"

"Yes," said Dickens easily, still not realizing that his words would drive his host beyond the brink, "and one other thing: I've been round at my publishers, poring with Chapman and Hall over the two versions of my manuscript. Now before their presses roll, they've asked me to make a last appeal to you to change your mind, sir."

"Change my ... You have ruined my career! My life! But for your infernal meddling ... That hideous reporter! *You* fetched him! You! You! You!"

141

"So Dickens did it!" Lord Pouncey cried accusingly. "He's a menace to society! Throw the blighter out!"

"By George, I think I will!" The more he thought about it, the more Cratchit found this a remarkably good idea. "That's all he's fit for! I *will* throw him out! This minute!"

"And I will help you, sir!" Pouncey and Cratchit grabbed Dickens's shoulders and arms. "The pleasure is mine! Out with him!"

"Gentlemen, I protest!" Dickens struggled vainly as they forced him to the door. "Do you really want to go down the ages as Algernon Muddlecombe? And you, Lord Pouncey, I shall see you're sued for this! With all the power of my pen I shall!"

"Be quiet, sir!" advised his lordship. "For once your words won't help you! So my speeches are promptly forgotten, are they? Well, you won't forget this one!"

Creep came up from his cubby-hole and decided to render all possible assistance. He opened the front door and rammed Dickens's hat on his head an instant before the young author was hurled out into the square.

"Good night, sir!" Lord Pouncey called mockingly as Dickens flew down to greet the pavement. "And good riddance!"

"And," shouted Bob Cratchit, not forgetting his manners or the season, "a merry Christmas!"

The two men, triumphantly dusting off their hands, turned and went back into the living-room. Creep was not done yet: perfect butler that he was, he noiselessly, efficiently, and calmly closed the front door.

Feeling much like one of his own put-upon heroes, Dickens ruefully studied, in an extremely close-up view, the snow-covered kerb and its neighbour, the gutter.

The door of his carriage opened, and Tessie Wither-spoon, deeply worried and clutching her face, climbed down to help him. Dickens's driver, Hoskins, also got down, and the two very quickly had Dickens on his feet.

The carriage's two black horses looked around specu-latively, but before they could plunge into a discussion as to what could possibly have happened, the carriage-door slammed, Hoskins cracked a whip across their backsides, and they were on their way.

George Gamester Bloggs, clerk to Messrs. Chapman and Hall, publishers, still had nothing to do—save, that is, watch the two worried Messrs. as they meandered and paced, then paced and meandered, up and down the front office of their distinguished publishing-house.

Chapman, the portly one, glanced at his pocket-watch and sighed. Hall, the thin one, looked at his partner and scowled. And "Gee-Gee" Bloggs, deep in gloom and becoming dizzy, rested his head on his hands and studied his desk.

The chief printer, Dudley Dugdale, entered the office in his black apron from the adjoining printing-house at the rear. And he came in backwards, for he had a different set of proofs in each hand. He looked at the partners expectantly. It was obvious from the manner in which his eyes blinked and his face twitched that he urgently wanted a decision: which script?

The Messrs. irritably waved him away. Dugdale re-turned to his printing-house, again backwards. "Gee-Gee" Bloggs, having eagerly looked up, now gazed through the front-office window and studied the gathering snow.

Pamphlet or no, Bloggs reflected, if they didn't start

soon, he would *never* get home in time to see his twelve children—or was it, he wondered, thirteen?—hang up their hopeful little stockings on this chilly Christmas Eve. He was glad now that he'd brought his topcoat after all.

"I enjoyed that," Lord Pouncey told Bob Cratchit for the umpteenth time—referring, of course, to the pair's brusque ejection of Dickens, "and you know, something that writer-fellow said just struck me: 'The power of the pen'."

"How so, my lord?" asked Cratchit, for he was a trifle naïve at times, as should now be well established.

"Write!" commanded Lord Pouncey imperiously. "That's it!"

Cratchit, who had been about to ask "How so, my lord?" a second time, decided against it for fear he might appear stupid, and instead he elected to look blankly at his lordship, which he did and did quite well.

"Write a letter," said Lord Pouncey, slapping Cratchit's hand, "telling the Prime Minister how that newspaper report actually came about. Blame Dickens—every politician worth his salt detests the man. Apologize to the hilt, and the Prime Minister may well be half-inclined to understand. Promise that Scrooge, if he lives, will never again be seen by any visitor to this house. Whine about your loyalty to the Prime Minister, flatter him, and remind him of your financial devotion to our noble party. And if you write such a letter, making Dickens out to be the only culprit, which he is, I shall deliver it to Number Ten Downing Street personally, this very night! It may well retrieve the situation! Perhaps even save it! Your knighthood is at stake! Your future!"

"Oh, *thank* you, my lord," said Cratchit obsequiously,

for even he had understood the gist of the plan. "I shall write at once, to your dictation. With your vast experience in these matters, I know perfectly well that you will know exactly what to say. Please come with me into the library."

And having indeed grasped the substance of Lord Pouncey's remarks, Cratchit now grasped his lordship's arm and steered him into the library and towards the escritoire.

A grim little procession turned into Mountjoy Square.

At its head was Mrs. Cratchit, her face flaked with snow. Next came Dr. Youngblood and Tiny Tim, and between them, on a blanket-shrouded stretcher, was the limp figure of Scrooge, of whom all that could be seen was the top of his new night-hat. Following them came Belinda, and bringing up the rear was Daisy Wellbeloved, who carried Scrooge's belongings like the good little maid she was.

Before going up the steps into the house, Mrs. Cratchit turned and raised a warning finger to her lips, motioning the others to be silent.

Hearing the library door close behind his master and Lord Pouncey, Creep had come up into the living-room and gone straight to the sideboard, where he was now helping himself to a generous swig of sherry, straight from the decanter, at the same time keeping one eye on the library, the other on the front door.

On seeing the front door open, Creep focussed his full attention on it. He replaced the decanter and hurriedly went over. "Mr. Scrooge! Oh, how is he, madam?"

"Sh! Sh!" Mrs. Cratchit sounded like an empty soda siphon. "Is Mr. Cratchit here?"

"In the library, madam."

"Drat!" She motioned the others to enter Scrooge's little cloakroom; all went in quietly. "Mr. Scrooge recovered consciousness briefly," she went on, answering Creep's question, "but only long enough to enquire if he might come home to die. I could not deny him that! Then he lapsed, the poor man, into unconsciousness again. Close that door, Creep; one of us shall remain with him to the end. At least he will not die lonely."

"Very good, madam." Sadly Creep lit Scrooge's oil-lamp, closed the cloakroom door, and took all bonnets, hats, and coats to the nearby rack. Daisy placed Scrooge's belongings in the drawers of a small cupboard and put the jar of potion, and the snuff-box that had been a present from Tiny Tim, on Scrooge's little bedside-table. His dressing-gown went back on its peg.

And Scrooge himself: he was lifted from the stretcher, his eyes still closed, his mouth slightly open, by Tiny Tim and Dr. Youngblood, placed in bed, and swiftly tucked in.

"Will he be all right," asked Mrs. Cratchit as the oil-lamp flickered its light over the assembled anxious faces and made large, quivering shadows on the walls, "at least for this evening, Doctor?"

"It was a good sign that he spoke, however briefly, madam," answered Youngblood, "but I think I should stay for some hours, if I may, in the event I am suddenly needed."

Belinda was close to tears. "Oh, must we fear the worst?"

"We can only pray," said Mrs. Cratchit, "that Mr. Scrooge has the will." She looked at the still head on its pillow. "Oh, there's no movement at all. He looks at death's door."

Tiny Tim suddenly cried, "May I stay with him, Mother? Please!"

"Yes, Tiny Tim . . . You have more right than any of us."

All froze. Their low conversation ceased. Loud and jovial voices could be heard, and they were coming, of course, from the living-room.

"A splendid letter!" exclaimed Lord Pouncey, holding up an envelope as he and Cratchit came in from the library. "A most brilliant letter, though I say it myself! I think this should prove just the ticket!"

"I am very grateful to you, my lord," said Cratchit, escorting Pouncey to the front door, where he handed him his things.

"Think nothing of it, sir! I shall present this at Number Ten forthwith! So much for Dickens—the bounder will be lucky if he sells another book! Good night to you!"

Cratchit opened the front door, and a swath of snow at once blew itself in, quite uninvited. "Good night, my lord. And thank you."

Pouncey braced himself and hurried out, still proudly holding up the vital letter addressed to the Prime Minister. Cratchit closed the door and rubbed his hands, well satisfied that at least he had a hope.

In Scrooge's room Mrs. Cratchit drew herself up, set her face, and determined that she would be the mistress of this delicate situation. She beckoned to the others to follow her, that is, with the exception of Tiny Tim, who sat close to Scrooge's bed, intently watching the old man. She now marched into the living-room with Creep and Daisy,

Belinda and Dr. Youngblood, close behind her. Creep closed Scrooge's door. Cratchit gaped on seeing the five troop in; in fact, he was astounded.

"Mrs. Cratchit, madam?!"

"Not a word, Mr. Cratchit, sir!" his wife responded firmly. "Mr. Scrooge is back at home where he belongs! Go downstairs, Creep and Daisy, and help Cook." The servants slipped away.

"Scrooge . . . Scrooge is in there now, against my orders?" Cratchit could not bring himself to believe it.

"Yes, and he is going to stay there, sir! You and I shall have a talk! Belinda, take Doctor Youngblood into the dining-room and keep him entertained!"

"Yes, Mother." And that's what Belinda and Youngblood did.

It must be said there was now a distinct movement in Scrooge's bed, and, not surprisingly, the movement came from Scrooge. He opened his eyes and, to Tiny Tim's intense delight, gave the boy a brave little smile.

Scrooge did more—he sat up! And more than that—he swung his legs from the bed and sat on its edge! And yet more—after admonishing Tiny Tim to remain quiet, he promptly helped himself to a spoonful of potion from the jar on his little bedside-table, and, as Tiny Tim rose and backed away in wonder, Scrooge rose, too, and took the boy's hand!

The two then tiptoed to the cloakroom door, where they listened to what Mr. and Mrs. Cratchit had to say in the living-room. Scrooge cupped a hand around his ear, though from time to time he used it to nurse and rub his painful throat, for Zachary Makepeace, the wicked turnkey of Paradise Hall, had done his work quite well, though

happily for us not quite well enough. Through the door
the bent old man and the young lad heard:

"Have you taken leave of your senses, woman?"

"No, sir, I have not!"

"And ... encouraging young people like that to talk
together, alone?"

"That doctor is perfectly honourable, sir, and so, if you
had but noticed it, is your remaining single daughter!"

"I do not want Scrooge in there! Not till I get my
knighthood! I have given the Prime Minister my word!"

"I have already informed Lord Pouncey that no
member of the Cratchit family has any desire to receive
any title whatever!"

"Is that so? Well, I wonder why he's just gone rushing
round to Downing Street with a letter from me, requesting
one! Abjectly apologizing, grovelling, pleading for another
chance, nay, begging for it on my knees!"

"Is this the Bob Cratchit I married? Is it?"

"And Scrooge will be out of that room the first thing
in the morning!"

"And so will I! Right out of this house!"

Scrooge held Tiny Tim's hand tightly. The two scarcely
dared to breathe. As for Bob Cratchit, his voice distinctly
faltered at the suggestion that his wife might go away.

"What? What are you saying, woman?"

"Move Mr. Scrooge, and I shall leave you. And what
will all your lords and ladies say then? Oh, remember your
beginnings, Bob!"

"I've been trying for seven years to forget them! You
can't leave me. You daren't!"

"I shall go back to our little terraced house in Camden
Town. The Johnstons will find me a room. One of *our* old
rooms."

Cratchit became rather emotional at the very idea. "You can't go back there! And on . . . Christmas Day . . . I'll not allow it, Alice . . . After all these years!"

"Then come into the library, sir, and you shall listen to my demands."

Tiny Tim considered that his mother was winning; Scrooge considered that she was not.

"Demands, madam? Am I no longer master in my own house?"

"No. Not if you wish me to remain here."

"Tish-tosh, madam! We shall see about that! Come with me!"

Tiny Tim now considered that his father was ahead, a verdict Scrooge not only shared but was convinced of. The two then heard the unmistakable crackle of paper: Mrs. Cratchit must have picked up her chocolate-box to give her solace and sustenance while her future was decided in the library.

"Oh, I almost forgot," they heard her say; and she added, not without a note of triumph, "you'll need these."

The library door closed behind them.

Scrooge went back to the bed and sat on it, worriedly rubbing his neck. His voice was very hoarse, like a broken saw. "Ah, that dear Mrs. Cratchit, she is the gem of this family. But what worries me, Tiny Tim, is, will she be able to persuade him?"

Tiny Tim was somewhat shaken, for he had never before in all his life heard his parents quarrel, and he was most upset to hear them do so now. But he could scarcely contain his joy and amazement on seeing that Scrooge had apparently recovered. "But Uncle Scrooge! You are all right!"

"I've taken harder blows than that, my boy," Scrooge

wheezed, "aye, and dealt 'em, too, in my time. I *did* lose wakefulness for a while—for a long while, too, I fancy—but I confess that for the past several hours I have been listening to all you dear, good people trying to help me."

Tiny Tim smiled and forgot his parents' bickering. "You were listening all along!"

"Ah, Tiny Tim," Scrooge croaked, "you will find when you grow old that the last deception of the elderly in this life is to pretend, my boy, *not* to be listening."

Scrooge now waxed expansive and spread out his thin arms.

"Ah, that wonderful man, Dickens! I heard him paying off, with what sounded like a mountain of gold, that awful hostelry-keeper, Axworthy, to secure my release and that of brave Tessie Witherspoon! And the terrible fate they have in store for that demented wretch, Zachary Make-peace, who lost his head and assaulted me! A terrible fate!" (Had Scrooge not gone into business as a young man, he would surely have made an outstanding actor—a great tragedian, in fact.)

"I didn't hear about that, sir," said Tiny Tim respect-fully. "What will they do to him?"

Scrooge had raised his bony hands to half-cover his face, and he now spoke through his fingers. "Confined to his quarters," he rasped dramatically, "until three p.m. on Christmas Day!" His hands slithered down like a broken portcullis; a charitable thought then caused him to brighten. "But I shall visit him, if I am well enough, on Christmas morning and take the poor, deranged fellow in his lonely cell a few little Christmas comforts. I know he'll be pleased to see me!"

And having given voice to this futile notion, Scrooge quickly got back into bed, tucked down his night-shirt, and pulled up the covers.

"And now, my boy, now that I am finally home, I must reluctantly engage in a further deception, just in case your mother is unable to convince your father that I should stay. Go and tell him, Tiny Tim," Scrooge deftly adjusted for effect his new night-hat so that its tassel flopped over his right eye, "go and tell him that I am a-dying and that I am calling for him. Tell him it appears I've been too long at the fair; he'll understand. Then stay in the library with your mother, and tell her that all is well."

Scrooge frowned. It seemed that Tiny Tim was doubtful about undertaking such a deceitful mission. "Hurry along, my boy."

"But you're not dying . . . are you?"

"I hope not."

"Then won't I be telling my father a lie?"

"Yes," Scrooge conceded impatiently, "but it's my belief that if you tell a small lie—"

"What, such as that you are *dying?*"

"If you tell it with the deliberate intention of helping someone, and you do help him, then I'm sure it's quite all right."

Scrooge sank back on his pillow and wondered what this persistent little perisher, whom he dearly loved, could possibly rejoin to that. His wait was short:

"Did you tell many lies when you were my age?"

"Thousands!" Scrooge heard himself half-shout the word, so he made his next remark subdued. "And not always to help others, I'm afraid."

"That's bad," Tiny Tim a shade too readily confirmed.

"It was rotten! And it was all because I thought too much about money. I was so obsessed with making lots of money that I forgot about everything else."

"Yes," Tiny Tim agreed, "Father often said you were

so greedy and grasping that you never found time to do the decent thing and find a wife. 'That,' he told us all on many occasions, "was undoubtedly his downfall and greatest tragedy.' "

Scrooge's old face twitched and his eyes narrowed. "Reach me," he commanded, "the rolled foolscap parchment you will find reposing at the back of that cupboard's drawer. I may need it."

Tiny Tim dutifully crouched, groped inside, and brought forth a dusty scroll tied with faded silver tapes. "Is this your last will and testament, sir?"

"No!" Scrooge snatched the document, dropped it in his bedside-table's drawer, and closed the drawer sharply. "Now run and fetch your father. Tell him I'm sinking so fast, I've probably scuttled myself."

"But—"

"And hurry up!" Scrooge cried. "My time is supposed to be short!" His shouts having hurt his throat, he controlled himself. "I mean," he added quietly, "kindly be swift."

Tiny Tim hurried out, leaving the door open. Scrooge pushed his glasses down his nose, rehearsed a few gasps, and practised several drawn-out groans while encouraging his face to fall in and his hands to droop forlornly. He wished he had a package of baking-flour handy, so that he might have licked his fingers, dipped them in the bag, and streaked the residue across his cheeks to give an onlooker the illusion of the presence of deathly paleness.

Oh, yes, as I have said, Scrooge would have made quite an actor, and he now prepared, as he waited in his little cloakroom, to give the performance of his life.

Lord Pouncey, with a hopeful smile, stood near the Prime

Minister's imposing desk at Number Ten Downing Street and watched as Sir Robert Peel read Cratchit's letter of apology.

A little off to one side—and Lord Pouncey had wondered what the devil the chap was doing there, but was much too polite to ask—there stood a stern-looking military man. He was resplendent in a magnificent uniform with large epaulets, a sword in its scabbard, gorgeous gauntlets, high boots, and silver spurs, and he held his splendidly plumed helmet in front of his much-bemedalled chest.

Lord Pouncey soon lost interest in the army officer—who later in this narrative will prove to be Captain Jason Lockhart and not at all the generalissimo Pouncey had taken him to be, but important to this account, as we shall see—and concentrated his attention on the Prime Minister, who, having twice read Cratchit's letter, was now in an ice-cold fury and quivering with rage.

To Lord Pouncey's mounting horror, and with awful deliberation, Sir Robert Peel slowly tore Cratchit's letter in half, reduced it to quarters, then to eighths, and finally allowed the remains to fall to the floor, watching them, as they fluttered, with grave fascination and not a little satisfaction. He then beckoned Captain Lockhart to step forward, which the officer did smartly, with a thump and a clink and a ready and willing jingle.

Bob Cratchit, now very anxious, hurried from the library. As he crossed the living-room to enter Scrooge's quarters, he stopped dead and paled.

"Send for Bob Cratchit!" he heard Scrooge call out hoarsely through the cloakroom's open door. "Only Bob Cratchit! My dying wish!"

To Cratchit's great credit, he forgot in that moment all about his business affairs and his standing in society. He went into the room and sat by the little bed as the old man looked up wanly. "I am here, Ebenezer."

"Take my hand, Bob! I'm going! Just a few last requests."

Memories of hard times and happy times poured into Cratchit's head as he touched and held the old man's languid hand. "But I had no idea you were so—"

"Promise me that you will never desert that good woman of yours!" Scrooge had to wait a few moments while Cratchit pondered this.

"Well, no, it's the other way around. She was just—"

"I knew you wouldn't, Bob!" Scrooge panted. "May I, may I stay here until I die? It will not be long. Please pledge to me your promise. Your solemn promise."

The appeal was so plaintive that Cratchit did not hesitate. "You have it, old friend." So Scrooge would die, and on Christmas Eve, of all the blessed evenings! Cratchit felt the need to produce his handkerchief; as he did, Scrooge glanced at him slyly and hoped he wouldn't have the bright idea of sending for Doctor Youngblood, whose name he was about to mention.

"And your dear daughter, Belinda," Scrooge puffed, "and that handsome doctor! Promise me that they may continue to see each other! They love each other!"

The sentimental thoughts that had flooded into Cratchit's brain just as suddenly receded. His lips formed an inverted u, then parted as he exclaimed peevishly, "I knew it!"

Scrooge slid his foot over to the pedal marked "Pitiful" in his gallery of organ-stops. "Don't make her marry someone old! And he's a brilliant boy, Bob, with a splendid future! He eased my gout, though too late for me to enjoy the relief. You'll find that all of fashionable London will flock to him . . . after I'm gone."

Cratchit blew his nose with the signal hoot of one of the railway's new fog-detonators. "I'll consider it, old chap."

"More." Scrooge's appeal sounded like a demand from his counting-house.

"Very well. I shall permit it. For a trial period."

Having wrung this concession, Scrooge now pushed his acting ability to the limit. He raised his head from the pillow, and, clutching at Cratchit's arm, he ignored his painful throat and shouted:

"And Tiny Tim! I know why he continues to be expelled! You persist in sending him to distant boarding-schools! When what he needs is love!"

"Love?" Cratchit repeated the word dully; but yes, he did have a definite recollection of the meaning of the word.

"Yes, love!" Scrooge pressed. "You must send him to a school near here so that he may live with you at home." He kicked the stop marked "Pathetic" and dropped his pitch a few tones. "He misses you, Bob, when you send him away. You must find more time for him and love him, too!"

The sight of Scrooge caring only for the welfare of others, even as he appeared to be writhing in his death-throes, touched Cratchit to the extent that he felt a sudden desire to dab at his eyes, which had become a trifle misty. "I will," he said emotionally.

But Scrooge desired more than this from his former clerk—aye, much more! Cratchit's eyes may have become cloudy as he sat there clenching his handkerchief, but by

Scrooge's reckoning he should have been near to tears a few impassioned appeals ago and in at least a slight lachrymose condition by now. But there was no evidence whatever, by way of a few sobs or a little weep, to indicate that Cratchit was even close to experiencing the joys of true repentance or that humility might yet be permitted to venture back into his heart. No, reflected Scrooge as he squinted at Bob's bone-dry face, his former clerk was merely waiting patiently for his mentor to die. No doubt he was already contemplating the difficulty of making funeral arrangements over Christmas, idly wondering whether Benjamin Tiptree and Son, obliged to bury a corpse during the holidays, might feel disposed to offer him their usual trade discount.

Scrooge decided it was now or never. The time had come to unleash his wiliest master-stroke in a bid to open Cratchit's tear-ducts, get those cerebral rivulets flowing, and so save him from himself. "And you, you yourself, Bob! Promise me you'll never change!"

The mention of his own important and good-natured personage caused Cratchit, not unnaturally, to be quite moved. "I promise," he sniffed. "You can rely on me. Always."

"Thank you, Bob. I should hate to see you take a turn for the worse by veering off the right track, as I did."

There was a slight pause, during which Scrooge rambled mindlessly, wriggling and squirming like a man in a coma and babbling almost incoherently—but not quite.

"What," asked Cratchit, and with good reason, "do you mean?"

"Don't let yourself become soft-hearted like me! Oh, I've watched your rigid and firm development, Bob, and not without pride!" Scrooge now tried rolling his eyes and gesturing vaguely. "Ah, that splendid fire of yours over there, giving out with that most brilliant blaze! See how it glows and flickers and flashes and flames!"

As there was no fireplace in sight, let alone a fire, Scrooge hoped Cratchit would conclude that his old partner's mind had slithered irretrievably over the brink into stultifying senility.

"I see it, old friend," Cratchit lied, wiping his eyes and letting his nose emit a small toot. "I see it well, Ebenezer."

"Now reach in that drawer, Bob, and hand me the roll of parchment you will find inside. I have one last task for you to perform just as soon as I am dead. One faithful, final job."

Cratchit opened the bedside-table's drawer and gave the scroll to Scrooge, who blew from its surface a little scud of fine dust and permitted himself a small coughing-fit. He then unravelled the silver tapes and unrolled the single page with a rasping crackle.

"Dozens of names here, Bob," Scrooge gasped as he examined his own spidery hand, "and you will remember them all. I want you to call on each one of these beggars and say my last wish was that I'd like my money back, please. Tell them before I died I had a last-minute change of heart. Explain that thanks to the wonderful lesson of life you taught me, I discovered that being generous does not pay. I think it will be appropriate, Bob, if you start collecting tomorrow."

"What lesson was that? And you want me to go out into the streets trying to scrape up money? For you, on Christmas Day?"

"For *you*. And that will be most timely, as you shall see. Look, Bob."

Cratchit took the page and gazed disbelievingly at names he had all but forgotten. He blinked as he scanned the large amounts of money that Scrooge had meticulously appended. The very sight of the two names that headed the list, "Ditheringham" and "Dobbs," had an instant effect—they carried Cratchit irresistibly back in time to the Christmas Eve of seven years before, back to his dismal cell outside Scrooge's office, where he sat and listened at his clerk's desk in the room known as "the Tank."

Ditheringham and Dobbs! Why, he himself had admitted them when they had come seeking funds to buy the poor and destitute some meat and drink and a little means of warmth on that freezing Christmas Eve! Their short visit had been in vain—Scrooge had quickly sent them packing—and he, Bob Cratchit, on ushering them out, had slipped Mr. Ditheringham, or perhaps it was Mr. Dobbs, all he could spare on his clerk's pay: a penny. Scrooge had then called him into his office, denounced him as mad for having let two such churlish pests into his presence, and threatened him with the sack. Cratchit vividly remembered returning to his desk and trembling as Scrooge's well-worn pen-nib scratched relentlessly and remorselessly on, resuming its never-ending quest to amass more money.

"Ditheringham and Dobbs!" Cratchit now exclaimed as Scrooge twitched in the bed and resorted to the most startling convulsions. "I cannot pursue these people! It's out of the question! Completely!"

"You must. You see, I relented a few days later and rashly gave the pair some cash. Tell them I now regard the sums that are recorded there not as donations but as loans. Insist that I want repayment of the amount that was advanced. Inform them that they are lucky, after seven long years, that I do not demand any interest! You will find their office on the corner of Paternoster Row and Grub Street. Top floor."

"I know I shall!" Cratchit expostulated. "But both men are unobtainable! Tobias Dobbs is dead, and he was followed three months later into Cripplegate Churchyard by his crony, Alfonso Ditheringham! I know, I refused to attend both their funerals! They both owed *me* money, too! For services not paid for!"

"What a pity," commiserated the still-wriggling Scrooge. "Now see who is next on the list. There must be a few who are still living out of the dozens on whom I frittered away my cash. Look at the names, Bob. Recite to me the names."

It is well worth recording—and therefore it shall be duly entered here—that it was at this moment, as he responded to Scrooge's bidding and scrutinized the various recipients and their establishments, that Cratchit began to feel, slowly at first but then with ever-increasing insistence, the pangs and aching throbs of both happy and sad remembrances. Why, he could put an anxious and pleading face to each and every one of those names! The endless and hopeful trudging down the years that had followed Scrooge's transformation, the oustretched hands, the clink of coins, always the rustle of banknotes at Christmas—and the merry laugh that invariably accompanied each gladly given gift! And now these same names and faces and hands seemed to quiver and leap from the page and tug at his very heart-strings as he heard himself read each scrawled entry aloud:

" 'Doctor Hollingsworth's Infirmary for the Aged in Hoxton Place.' "

"Is Hollingsworth still alive?"

"Afraid not."

"No point in trying him then. What's the next entry say?"

" 'Oldacre's Dispensary for the Whitechapel Paupers.' "

"What about Oldacre?"

"Gone two years ago."

"I wondered why he stopped coming around. Carry on. This is becoming exciting. And interesting. And somewhat irritating."

" 'Brigadier Manley's Home for Disabled Soldiers and Sailors at Richmond Bridge.' "

"Dead?"

"No. Demolished."

"Blast. Brigadier Manley touched me to the quick. Continue."

" 'Mrs. Goddard's Hostelry for Orphaned and Unwanted Children in Turnpike Lane.' "

"I must have *built* that hostelry, brick by expensive brick."

"Sold last year. It's now a boot factory."

"Another wasted effort! I'm beginning to shake. Proceed."

The names began to swim and blur as Cratchit reviewed the prodigious parade of the old man's munificence, and all to the accompaniment, from the fitful benefactor in the bed, of the most rabid groans and fierce contortions. Here they all were, and the more Scrooge deplored his own largesse and cried out to be reimbursed, the more Cratchit was affected by the moving record:

" 'Sir William Launchbury's Yuletide Gifts of Edibles, Old Apparel, and Fuel for the Needy—' "

"There's one you can try! Sir William is still at it! The old nuisance was here only last week, collecting again! Tell him I'm the needy one now! Who's next?"

" 'Archdeacon Moodie's Christmas Fund for Impover-ished and Deserving Gentlefolk—' "

"Tell the archdeacon I lost my faith in Christmas after you tried to send me away. Now I don't have to keep it any more."

"Please don't say that. You make me feel so terribly—"

"On the contrary! I commend you, Bob, on your fine example and strength of character—and heartily so! Now kindly press on, I'm beginning to feel quite dizzy. I think I'm shivering, too."

" 'Barlow's Discreet and Refined Funerals for Chris-tians who Pass Out of this World in Penury.' "

"You should use George Barlow for me, Bob! I'm sure he will be glad to bury me for nothing after everything I've given him! You will save a pretty penny."

"Oh, Ebenezer, can't you see? I don't want to save on anything like that. Look at me. Don't want it to happen."

"Oh, but you must save. It pleases me to think you'll remain consistent after I'm gone. Now look back at that list and tell me about my next mistake. You know, this is proving to be nothing less than a litany of my most colossal and costly blunders. But why are you hesitating, Bob? Please do hurry."

" 'Doctor Ernst . . .' "

"Who?"

" 'Doctor Ernst . . .' I can't see it."

"Can't *see* it, d'you mean, or can't *say* it?"

"Both, I'm afraid."

"I've never heard of any Doctor Ernst! Never, ever!"

"Yes, you have. You know you have."

"Stop twitting and tantalizing me! Can't you see I'm dying? Read!"

" 'Doctor Ernst Wunderkind of Geneva, Switzerland,

for Treatment, at his Sanitarium and Spa, of ... Master Tim.'"

"Oh, *him?*"

"I do confess I'd almost forgotten. And may God bless you indeed for what you did, Ebenezer! I shall always be so grateful for that."

It was here, to Scrooge's intense but secret relief, that a lone tear, which must have been biding its time all along and waiting for its cue to make an entrance, finally ventured out to make its presence felt, slipped and lost its balance, veered down Cratchit's face, dribbled past his trembling lips, used his chin for a ski-jump, and fell softly and lightly onto the faded parchment. Yet this damp and irrefutable evidence that Cratchit did harbour feelings of human sentiment after all still wasn't enough for Scrooge, who now did his best to make light of the entire and long-forgotten medical transaction:

"Doctor Wunderkind, you say? Yes, well, he can keep what *he* received, no point in hounding him. After all, have you ever tried getting money back from a doctor? Medicos don't give refunds, not even when their patients die—especially not then. Besides, Doctor Wunderkind is abroad, he's far too far away for you to get at. Now find me a debtor who's hereabouts in this vicinity! Look hard and look sharp! I'm beginning to feel quite faint!"

Cratchit unrolled the parchment to its fullest extent until he found someone who lived close by. The particular recipient he came upon was entered not once but several times, and on seeing the name he gave a start of recognition. And when he announced the beneficiary's identity, he felt his voice vibrate and his heart move over to take up determined and pulsating residence in his throat:

" 'R. Cratchit ... for the Purchase of a Terraced Dwelling-House ... at Number Seventeen, Mercer's Row, Camden Town.' "

Upon hearing, at last, this mention of Cratchit himself, Scrooge employed the audacious tack he'd been holding in reserve. He plunged into what he hoped would pass for delirium, making out by his inane chatter that the Bob Cratchit who now sat gulping fretfully by his bed had nothing whatever to do with the boorish person on the list. He pretended they were as discrete as chalk and cheese.

"Let him have the house and welcome to it! You'll never get anything back from that one! He's overdrawn at the memory bank!"

"But didn't you hear? That's—"

"Stay right away from him, I'm warning you! Now tell me about my next disaster!"

" 'R. Cratchit ... to Provide for a Fund for the Education of Peter, Martha, Belinda, and Timothy Cratchit, his Four Children.' "

"And the ingrate wouldn't let me say good-bye to one of them! Before packing me off to a home! I forget when it happened. I can't think."

"But you're talking about—"

"I rue the day I ever plucked him from the rabble of the unemployed! Now jog me with my next catastrophe!"

" 'R. Cratchit ... to Secure for him Full Membership in the Stock Exchange.' "

"This one I do remember! That's when he tipped up the shafts of his memory-wagon! He let the whole cartload of his indebtedness slide off into the dust! Dumped it there! You should avoid him like the plague!"

"You're absolutely right to think so little of me. I did become hard when I joined the Exchange. That's when it started, it all went to my head. I can't deny it. I admit it, Ebenezer."

"What's that? Kindly stop mumbling and get on with your fossicking!"

" 'R. Cratchit . . .' "

"There he is again! He's taunting me, tormenting me! That man should have been arrested long ago for flagrant importuning and held without bail for flagitious neglect! What was I stupid enough to do for that walking tragedy this time? Answer me straight out!"

"You paid for his entrance into the Cock Tavern Mercantile Club. Made him a member for life."

"And for once I did right! I presented those parasites with their meanest member in the club's history! After me."

"Please don't make me read to you any more."

"But there's only one entry left, isn't there? An important one. Foot of the page, I fancy."

"So you do know what's written here after all."

"What I mean to say is—and providing my retentiveness isn't entirely unhinged—I believe you will find one remaining example of my misguided generosity. Remind me what I did so I can try to remember to forget it. Unless you consider recounting my greatest blunder too much to your distaste . . . Well?"

" 'R. Cratchit . . .' "

"Yes?"

" '. . . to Acquire for him a Full Partnership . . .' "

"Go on."

" '. . . that will be Legal and Binding . . .' "

"You want me to finish it for you? '. . . in the Firm of Scrooge and Marley.' There! And he went on to botch his life. I am so disappointed."

"Oh, Ebenezer . . ."

Scrooge sank back, closed his eyes, stopped twitching—and was rewarded with a single sob. It was everything he'd been waiting and hoping to hear, and it told
him it was time to speak quietly and in terms of
mitigation. Why, it was almost as though he might have
been misjudging this "R. Cratchit" fellow all along:

"Of course, it was not entirely his fault. Perhaps I
pushed him up the ladder too fast. He got caught in a
terrible scramble, in a race that hardens the hearts of the
gentlest of men and makes them shallow and impenitent,
callous and cruel. He forgot that grabbing for material
things and legitimate profit does not necessarily mean
one must lose one's principles in the chase. Why, things
are becoming so bad in the headlong rush and onslaught
of our modern society, I wonder the churches don't
complain! So who can be surprised that this Cratchit,
trammelled most of his life by restrictions of opportunity,
suddenly gave vent to his initiative? He began to live
ahead of the moment, beyond the minute, in his struggle
for gain. My only regret is that he forgot his former
poverty, his friends, and his family's love."

Scrooge heard a second sob. Encouraged by this, he
kept his eyes closed and went on, "I finally feel as if I may
be ... slipping away."

"Take my hand! Please!" And Cratchit blurted out the
words that Scrooge had been longing for. "Can you—can
you ever forgive an old fool who didn't have eyes to see or
ears to hear? Can you find it in your heart to forgive me?
Can you, Ebenezer? I've been so cruel to you. Please live,
and I'll change! For the better, I promise. But don't die.
You just have to give me one more chance."

"I suddenly feel ... terribly cold."

"Oh, no! Not yet."

Scrooge opened his eyes, saw a caring face streaked

with tears, and decided to counter his former clerk's mournful tones by pressing joyfully on all the organ-stops in his keyboard's gallery to deliver a veritable antiphon of arpeggios, brightly played.

"Yes, I'm terribly cold!" Scrooge exulted, smiling and whipping off the bed-covers. "Will you be kind enough to pass me my dressing-gown? I think I shall go into the living-room and warm myself by your glorious fire! Oh, I know there's no fire in here, never was, and that's why I'm shivering! You're not going to help me into my dressing-gown? Very well, sir, I shall put it on myself!"

Scrooge sprang from the bed. Cratchit gaped like one of Queen Victoria's new Royal Mail letter-boxes. "You . . . But you can't! . . . Oh, Ebenezer, you've been . . . You're not going to die?"

"No, but when I do, I shall die happy! You're a conversion for our times, Bob, a joyous reaffirmation that hearth and home and friends and fireside are the only values that really count! Oh, I don't want any money back from those dear people! Give me that list—I only kept it because sometimes I liked to look at it. But now I don't need it any more! I have what's better—your kind affection again!"

Scrooge snatched the parchment and tore it apart! He threw the pieces in the air! As for Cratchit's amazement, it was quickly replaced by a wide, warm smile; his relief was so great that more tears began to flow! To conceal them he rose and stood behind Scrooge, helping him into his robe.

"Now look here," Cratchit said reproachfully, "you gave me a nasty moment then, I thought I'd lost you. Never do that again, old man."

"Ah, Bob, I know you are not one to harbour grudges or hoard any slights, but I ask you to forgive me for causing you undue anxiety. And I promise that the next time I do such a thing, I shall be truly dying, my warrant on it! Now hurry along, old fellow, and I shall open my new snuff-box so we may share a pinch or two! And I should like some rum," Scrooge chirpily instructed his former clerk as he peregrinated rapidly around his tiny quarters, "hot rum, and ask Mrs. Summerhayes to send up several of her delicious mince-pies—I'm peckish! Oh, I'm so glad I've transformed you, Bob, and just in time for Christmas! You'll be surprised, my friend, how long the feeling lasts! So now then, Mister R. Cratchit, or Robert, or better yet, Bob—to the fireside!"

Scrooge seemed to know that Cratchit had best be left alone for a moment, so he nimbly stooped and picked up his slippers, took his new snuff-box, and went quickly into the living-room.

It goes without saying—but perhaps it had better be said—that Cratchit cared not a jot for his title any more. He repaired his tear-streaked features and reflected that all that mattered now was that Mr. Scrooge would be all right and that the Cratchit family, along with their faithful benefactor, would enjoy not only another merry Christmas, but also their merriest in years.

As he slowly followed Scrooge into the living-room, Cratchit suddenly remembered that he had made certain promises that Scrooge would expect him to keep. He made up his mind to honour each one of them—indeed, to see them all fulfilled within the hour!

Down in the kitchen that most excellent cook, Mrs. Ariadne Summerhayes, slid her famous mince-pies into the oven, then rose to give Creep and Daisy a final going-over.

Daisy held a tray filled with glasses. Creep swayed, holding, as he did, a tray containing a large and steaming bowl of potent punch.

Mrs. Summerhayes frowned. She took Creep's tray and put it on the table, grabbed Daisy's tray and gave it to Creep, picked up Creep's tray and handed it to Daisy, then put her hands to her worried face and shook her head as the two pushed off and approached the steep servants' stairway.

Cratchit strode to the library and threw open the door. "Come, my love! Timothy!" he called out cheerfully. "Mr. Scrooge is feeling much, much better!" He hurried to the dining-room and opened the door. "Doctor Youngblood! Belinda! Please come in! It's wonderful news!"

The four came in, all smiles, and headed for the fireplace, where Scrooge, with some concern, was looking up at Queen Victoria's portrait. "Oh, how I've changed!" he exclaimed.

Cratchit promised fervently, "And it will be changed right back, Ebenezer!"

Scrooge sat in Cratchit's favourite armchair and put on his slippers; Tiny Tim sat on the chair's arm and watched with relief and pleasure as his father kissed his mother with affection. Creep and Daisy ventured over with their trays.

"Oh, may I serve, sir?" Creep asked anxiously. "May I be reinstated?"

"No, you may not serve!" said Cratchit testily. He took the tray from the butler's hands. "*I'll* serve," he said with a smile. "*You* may sit down. And for wrecking my carriage, you shall have an increase in salary! I never liked that carriage, anyway. The man who made it fled to America."

Creep nearly fell into a chair. "Oh, thank you, sir!"

Mrs. Cratchit was radiant. "And I shall take Daisy's tray! May I, Bob?"

"Yes, my love, you may do anything you want! And Daisy, your salary will also be immediately increased. Sit down, my girl."

"God bless you, guv'nor!" And Daisy sat.

As Cratchit and his wife moved around with the drinks, Scrooge chose the moment to remark, to no one in particular, "I've been through all this before, you know! It's positively exhilarating, isn't it?"

Creep raised his glass of punch and announced mendaciously, though everyone instantly forgave him, "My first today!"

Scrooge's former housekeeper, Mrs. Henrietta Gubbins, came huffing and puffing and waddling into Mountjoy Square at speed, her black hat white with snow.

She had gone with Scrooge and the others from Paradise Hall to Doctor Lovejoy's clinic and had then returned to Mincing Lane to deal out the cards, gaze at the ball, and read the tea-leaves in a bid to discover whether Scrooge would pull through.

The indications had been good, and, as we shall see, she also learned something concerning her own immediate future that would affect her designs on Mr. Scrooge. She banged on the Cratchits' door, eager to know if the signs had been right.

Belinda Cratchit, who had of course been sitting next to Dr. Youngblood, ran to the door and opened it.

"Oh!" said Mrs. Gubbins anxiously as she stepped in. " 'Ow's Mr. Scrooge?"

Belinda smiled, nodded in the direction of the living-room, and took Mrs. Gubbins's hat and coat. Mrs. Gubbins followed Belinda's gaze and gave a cry of delight. "Oh, Mr. Scrooge! You're lookin' well again! Fair warms me cockles!" She strode across the room and kissed Scrooge on the forehead.

Cratchit was ready with the punch-tray. "Have a punch, Mrs. Gubbins," Cratchit said, "and please join us."

"Well, thank you, sir." She took a glass and stared at Scrooge. "But look at you, Mr. Scrooge, yer 'alf undressed!"

"All is pure to the pure in heart, Mrs. Gubbins, but I have to tell you I shall never become your fifth."

"Oh, don't worry about that, I've bin readin' the tea-leaves, an' accordin' to the cup I read this evenin', love, me next'll be an undertaker."

"So," said Scrooge, cheerfully raising his glass, "will mine, I rather fancy!"

Bob Cratchit saw, to his pleasure and satisfaction, that everyone except himself was now sitting round the fire and nursing a glass. He decided that the moment had come to make a little speech to the company, so he stood with his back to the fire to command attention, then hoisted his own glass and cleared his throat.

"And finally, everyone," he began, "a Christmas toast. No, not yet, Creep. It is seven years now since Mr. Scrooge heard me propose the health of the Founder of the Feast."

A wistful look at once glazed over Scrooge's eyes, and he gave a little smile.

"Well, I meant *him*," Cratchit went on, "and tonight, again, I mean *him*. To Mr. Scrooge, above all." He turned to the young lovers, remembering his promise to Scrooge. "To Belinda and Dr. Youngblood, without, of course, giving them undue encouragement, may love truly find a way"—the two promptly held hands; then he turned to his wife—"as it has with me and my own devoted wife, dear Mrs. Cratchit."

Mrs. Cratchit gave a shy and delighted smile as her husband turned to Tiny Tim.

"To Tiny Tim—and I think I shall start calling you that again, my boy, I prefer it for you, I really do—"

"Oh, *yes*, Father!" beamed Tiny Tim. "Please do!"

"—never again will I send him off to distant schools in remote parts of England. He shall stay here with us in the bosom of his family"—Scrooge and Tiny Tim exchanged happy glances as Cratchit went on—"for I see no reason at all why he shouldn't be expelled from *London* schools for a change. And as for me, personally, I promise in future to be—"

"Hurry up, Bob," said Scrooge, who noticed that Creep was fidgeting. "My punch is growing impatient."

"I sincerely promise that I shall remember always to—"

But Cratchit was again interrupted, this time by someone pounding on the door with what proved, when Tiny Tim had darted over and opened it, to be a silver-topped stick.

Lord Pouncey, very flustered and brushing snow from his sleeves, stepped inside and gave his hat to Tiny Tim, who stood and gazed out through the open door at someone who was still outside on the step.

"Mr. Cratchit!" Lord Pouncey called. "Forgive me for intruding, but I gave your most important letter to the Prime Minister—and he tore it up!"

"Oh, no, my lord," said Cratchit, who no longer cared. "Didn't he read it?"

"Read it twice! His face froze, and then he ripped it to shreds! And here, Mr. Cratchit, is the reason!"

Pouncey beckoned forward the stern-looking military man whom we met in the Prime Minister's office, and as he came clanking in, in all his colourful glory—which is to say, in his magnificently plumed helmet, dazzling uniform, splashy epaulets, gleaming sword-top, showy scabbard, swish gauntlets, flashy thigh-high boots, shining medals, not forgetting his jingling spurs, and I mention his accessories again merely to refresh your vivid memory of him—well! The entire company—which is to say, and I mention their names to you only to remind you that they were present: Scrooge, Mr. and Mrs. Cratchit, Belinda and Dr. Youngblood, Mrs. Gubbins, Creep and Daisy, Tiny Tim, and, of course, Lord Pouncey himself, who now cried "Captain Lockhart!" in ringing tones—stared in wonderment at the spectacle of it all, for nothing like this had ever been seen in the Cratchit living-room before, and Captain Lockhart, as he marched purposefully to the fireplace, did not even have the courtesy to remove his helmet, either, something they must have forgotten to tell him about at officers' training school.

Scrooge was the first to speak, and what he said, as Tiny Tim closed the door and ran back to his place on the arm of Scrooge's chair, was full of grim foreboding yet laced with just a touch of glee, "Good gracious me! They've come to *arrest* you, Bob!"

Captain Lockhart, iron-faced, had a voice of steel to match. He looked around at the assembled, staring company, then icily demanded, "Have I the honour of addressing one Ebenezer Scrooge?"

"Oh, it's *me* he wants!" cried Scrooge, rising. "All right, I surrender! But I must say I didn't expect anything like this to happen, not on Christmas Eve! Oh dear, he has a warrant!"

Captain Lockhart was indeed pulling a scroll of

parchment from the inside of his tunic, and he now addressed himself to Scrooge in the gravest tone. "Did you send this morning, by means of a common errand-boy, a jar of potion to the most illustrious household in the land?"

"Yes, I did!" Scrooge cried, "I sent Doctor Youngblood's *other* jar of potion! He gave me two, you see. I sent a boy I met seven years ago!"

"Then I am commanded to read to you this letter."

"Give it to me," said Scrooge impatiently. "I'll read it. Don't need you to read—"

"No, *I'll* read," said the splendid officer. "It is in the hand of Her Gracious Majesty herself."

Cratchit exclaimed, "Queen Victoria?!"

Captain Lockhart cleared his throat as though he were about to sing the national anthem or "Land of Hope and Glory" or a combination of both at the same time.

"Dear Mr. E. F. Scrooge," he began, his voice going up approximately half an octave in a fair impersonation of the Queen's voice, as her portrait on the wall behind him gazed majestically down. "We have commanded the officer who bears this letter to proceed to the Prime Minister's residence and thence to you, as the potion that you kindly sent to us this morning has greatly relieved our gout."

Scrooge gave a bashful smile as the officer continued.

"We also desire to be acquainted with the doctor whose name appears upon the label."

Youngblood flushed with pleasure and held on tightly to Miss Belinda's hand.

"And the Prime Minister," Captain Lockhart went on grandly, "has been informed of our intention to confer upon you, Mr. Scrooge, our personal bestowal of a knighthood"—Scrooge's jaw collapsed and his eyebrows jumped—"in appreciation of your splendid gesture. Signed, Victoria Regina. P.S. Prince Albert thanks you, too, and says all is forgiven."

Lord Pouncey, grinning hugely, thumped Cratchit hard. "And the Prime Minister says," his lordship crowed, "that if Mr. Scrooge can get one, you can have yours, too!"

Scrooge threw out his arms and marched triumphantly over to Cratchit.

"Sir Robert!" Scrooge exclaimed.

"Sir Ebenezer!" Cratchit cried.

The two embraced, which is hardly surprising, since each had his hands and arms outstretched and had every intention of effusively congratulating and hugging the other.

A wave of delight swept the company. Only now did Captain Lockhart remove his headgear and smile; he and Lord Pouncey then gratefully accepted drinks from Mrs. Cratchit's tray. And in this glorious moment Scrooge did not forget Tiny Tim. He picked him up and swung him around until his feet left the floor. And then Scrooge addressed the boy confidentially—it was almost as if the others were not present at all:

"Well, now, Tiny Tim, it appears we have a happy ending after all. And I believe, my boy, that on this festive occasion you, more than any of us, know exactly what to say."

Tiny Tim fairly squirmed with embarrassment. He looked up into Scrooge's lined and beaming features and replied, very awkwardly, "Oh, no, Uncle Scrooge, I couldn't. I couldn't say it, I couldn't!"

"Well, come on," Scrooge said, turning to the others and holding out his free hand. "Let's all say it. Shall we say it for Tiny Tim? Come on—one, two, three."

And Scrooge, and Bob Cratchit, and Mrs. Cratchit, and Belinda, and even Tiny Tim all loudly called: "God bless us, every one!" for this earnest wish had been a favourite saying of the entire Cratchit family for many a long and blessed year.

Scrooge was just taking Tiny Tim back to the armchair when there was a thunderous burst of knocking on the front door.

Tiny Tim asked innocently, "Who the dickens can *that* be?"

"I'll give you one guess, my boy!" Scrooge answered with a knowing laugh. "One only!"

Creep decided that he would open the door this time, and he staggered, this way and that in a most unbutler-like fashion, until he performed the feat. Dickens was there, in his hat and cape, looking like the abominable snowman. Very anxious and beside himself with frustration, he came striding in, holding up a pamphlet with bright new covers. Cratchit came forward to greet him.

"My dear Mr. Cratchit, sir," said Dickens, waving the pamphlet in Cratchit's surprised face. "I'm terribly sorry to disturb you at such a late hour, but something dreadful has happened! Chapman and Hall have published *A Christmas Carol*, but the idiots have printed the *wrong manuscript*, the one in which you are you and Mr. Scrooge is Mr. Scrooge! A typographical blunder of the first magnitude!"

Cratchit smiled, placed his hand on Dickens's shoulder, and took him to join the others at the fireside as Dickens jabbered on. "So you see, Mr. Cratchit," he said, gesturing wildly, "I really must implore you for permission to use the actual names. I'm begging you, beseeching you ..."

The young author's voice trailed off. He discovered,

first to his consternation, then to his growing delight, that he was surrounded by a sea of the most shining and receptive and accommodating faces! Even Queen Victoria, from her place high on the wall, seemed for once to look down on him benignly.

There never was such a clatter—such a shake and rattle, thud and thump—as the printing presses on the premises of Messrs. Chapman and Hall, publishers, went about their mighty and enlightening business.

The front office was now the scene of almost feverish activity as George Gamester Bloggs, clerk to the Messrs., doled out stacks of just-printed pamphlets to a line of eager drifters, derelicts, and down-and-outs who had been recruited to sell them on commission. The clanking and thundering swelled as Dudley Dugdale, the chief printer, again came in backwards from his printing-house, and this time his apron was piled with hundreds more of the little booklets, for Dickens, in his kindly wisdom, had insisted that the first edition of his Christmas story be printed cheaply. He had done this, not with any sordid thought that he might gain, but in the hope that the poor would be able to afford it and, perhaps, be cheered and heartened thereby.

Two silhouettes—one stout, one lean—could again be seen on the front office's frosted-glass partition, and behind it, judging by Mr. Chapman's elated delivery as he read the pamphlet's final page to his partner, Mr. Hall, it appeared that he considered they had brought off a coup of some sort—a daring publishing coup, no less. He read out proudly:

" 'Make up the fires, and buy another coal-scuttle before you dot another i, Bob Cratchit!' "

Mr. Chapman smiled. Mr. Hall got his handkerchief ready.

"Scrooge," went on Mr. Hall's portly partner, "was better than his word. He did it all, and infinitely more; and to Tiny Tim, who did NOT die—"

Mr. Hall dabbed at his eyes and smiled with relief and pleasure, not knowing that countless millions all over the world would in years to come do exactly the same.

"—he was a second father. He became as good a friend, as good a master, and as good a man, as the good old city knew, or any other good old city, town, or borough in the good old world."

As Mr. Chapman went on to read the final, immortal lines, outside in the front office "Gee-Gee" Bloggs handed a stack of pamphlets to a young man of about eighteen whose turn it now was, and by the happiest chance, it was the same young man, in his sloppy cap and shabby clothes, to whom Scrooge had entrusted the little jar of potion to be delivered to the Queen.

The young man went quickly into the street, for he was anxious to earn some Christmas money, and his voice mingled with other leather-throated voices, calling: "New work by Mr. Dickens! New story for Christmas! Cheap edition now on sale!"

The hawkers of the first edition of *A Christmas Carol* hurried off into the snow.

Helped by three stalwart Puddle Dock policemen and by several swearing members of the Blackfriars Bridge fire brigade, Eustace Fonsdale, Bob Cratchit's driver, hacked away at his master's ruined carriage, kicked what was left, and sent the remains cruising down the river.

As Fonsdale trudged up Bow Street on the way to

THE CALAMITY RESOLVED

Mountjoy Square, he heard the shouts of the pamphlet-vendors but paid them no heed. All that mattered was that his long-sought companion, now silent and subdued, was hungry and weary and longing for his stable and his manger on this wintry Christmas Eve.

Hercules was going home.

THE END